THE RANCHER'S SECOND CHANCE

Parker Ranches, Inc.

Book 1

MADDIE JAMES

The Rancher's Second Chance

Rock Creek Ranch, Book 1

When John Rankin's wife dies, leaving him with two children to raise, he wonders how he can he take care of a family and run a working cattle ranch, too. Annie's domain was home, hearth, and the kids. Her dying put a hole in his day-to-day existence like nothing he'd ever before experienced—not only in his rancher lifestyle, but also in his heart.

As the months roll on, his heart is only one of his problems when eleven-year-old Callie rebels. Missing her mom and unsure how her life is unfolding, Callie pushes back at every turn, and John is unsure how to help her. Then his friend and farm manager, Buck McGinnis, suggests John seek the counsel of a woman for advice dealing with a moody pre-teen female. He wants to introduce John to his friend, Abby Cooper.

John is reluctant, but eventually caves to Buck's advice.

Suddenly, life becomes more complicated.

The Parker Ranches

Whether working the cattle ranch, or the dude ranch side of the business, the Rankin family is firmly rooted into their Montana ranching way of life. It's not easy. Relationships get in the way. Egos sometimes, too. But at the very core of their existence, is home, family, and love.

Linked by strong family relationships, these stories take place in multiple ranch settings in Montana (Rankin's Rock Creek Ranch; The Branded Filly Ranch).

When Gage Parker of Billings seeks to add to his business portfolio, he decides to branch out into a world he knows well. Hotels are his business but ranching is in his blood. The addition of a South Dakota ranch into his conglomerate increases not only his land holdings but expands his family.

The Parker and Rankin families—Montana ranchers for generations—anchor the series and lay the foundation for stories to come. As families grow, forming new ranch partnerships, you'll also meet the MacKay and Remington families, among others.

These books are romance stories with happily-ever-after endings. Some are sweet, most are steamy, and a few are romantically erotic.

Prologue

*S**ummer, 1978*

JOHN RANKIN SLOWLY EXITED HIS TRUCK, GLANCING BACK AT his horse trailer hitched behind it. It felt good to stretch his legs after driving for hours. Facing ahead, he parked his fists on his hips and stared up at the Parker Ranch sign. Been a few years since he'd crossed under that piece of wood—the name of the ranch burned into it like a brand—but he was about to do that in a few minutes. The sign had taken a beating over the years, the words faded from sun and wind, but he knew he was in the right place.

How long had it been? Nearly a decade?

Taking a deep breath, he held it, like he knew when he let it out, his life would change.

Some sort of premonition? Hell, he didn't know if he believed in that shit. What would be, would be, was his motto. Over the years, he'd learned to take life one day at a time.

His gaze shifted to another makeshift sign on the fence post next to the road, the words WRANGLERS WANTED scrawled on the piece of cardboard.

Well, he was a wrangler, and he needed work, that was for certain. If he'd be wanted or not, he guessed he'd find out. His last ranch was in Idaho. The fight with the rancher's son was the reason he got kicked off that piece of land. Too bad the kid got his arm broken in the ruckus, but he'd warned the little son-of-a-bitch to keep his distance and stay away from his girl.

He didn't.

So, John headed home to Montana—leaving the Idaho ranch and his cheating girlfriend behind. It remained to be seen if coming home would be a good idea. His buddy, Tom—his last connection with anyone back in Paradise Valley—told him his father was looking for ranch hands. Thought he might as well try it, even though Tom Parker, Sr. had told him years ago he was no longer welcome on his ranch.

Slowly, he eased out that breath he'd been holding.

Motion off to his right caught his eye. A horse and rider burst over the hill and upon seeing him, pulled up to a halt. The rider held a hand to their eyes and stared his way. In a blink, heels booted the horse's sides, and they took off toward him.

As they galloped closer, he could see that the rider was a woman. She pulled up short in front of him.

"Can I help you?"

The whip of a woman couldn't be more than seventeen. Her blond hair, caught up in a long messy ponytail, trailed down her back. She was every inch a cowgirl, from her frayed Wranglers to the tip of her dusty boots. John imagined if she stood facing him, she'd maybe come up to his chest, perhaps no taller than five-foot-two—even with her boots on.

Her horse pranced while she expertly balanced herself in the saddle.

"Well? Can you speak?"

John chuckled. "Yes, I can speak. I'm looking for work. Mr. Parker in today? I'm a friend of his son, Tom Jr."

Her gaze narrowed. She stared for a heartbeat, then tipped her head and frowned. Her hat shadowed her eyes, but he saw a brief flash of blue.

"You're friends with my brother? How come I don't know you?"

John paused for a second or two. "Annie Parker?"

She nodded. "I am. Who are you?"

"John Rankin," he replied. "I went to school with Tom but left before we graduated. I've been working ranches out of state. Thought I'd come back home. You've grown up." He remembered her from a decade earlier when he and Tom and Cody Reynolds were tight—an inseparable trio that got in too much trouble. She might have been nine or ten back then.

"People do that. Grow up. I sort of remember you." She tugged at her horse's reins, pulling at the bit. The horse backed up a little and danced. "Dad's up in the barn working on the baler. He could use some help this time of year." A smirky smile crossed her face. "That is, if you're up to dirty work, long days, and no time off, cowboy."

In the next instant, she left, before he could utter a quick comeback. John watched the dust billow up behind her as she galloped up the dirt road and over the hill, where he knew the ranch house and barns and outbuildings sat.

"Hell fire." John exhaled the words. "Little Annie Parker. All grown up." Suddenly, he wasn't sure if working here was a good idea. Her snarky grin had sent his heart into a brief gallop. Not good. He should leave.

His heart wasn't ready to be toyed with again so soon.

Besides, there were plenty of ranches in the area—ones that didn't come with the temptation of the rancher's daughter —and usually they could all use an extra hand.

Besides, she was way too young for him.

He glanced again at the WRANGLERS WANTED sign. *One day at a time, Rankin. Today, you need a job, and they got work.* He got back in his truck and headed up the hill.

TOM PARKER, SR. HAD HIS BACK TO HIM, REACHING INTO THE guts of the hay baler when John stepped inside the barn. One wheel removed from the implement, the older man was halfway into and underneath the machine. Tom didn't acknowledge his presence. John didn't know if the rancher knew he was anywhere near, so he kept quiet standing a few feet behind him until his eyes fully adjusted to the shadows in the barn, waiting until the senior Parker finished fiddling with the thing. Or until he stepped away and faced John. Whichever came first.

But neither happened. Tom Parker twisted something with his right arm while holding something else steady with his left. Suddenly, he barked out, "Hand me that wrench over there. Will you?"

John glanced at the workbench to his right, took a step toward it, spotted the wrench, and handed it to him.

"Thanks." The guy never looked up. He fiddled with the wrench for a while. "My father had this philosophy that if you can fix it, you don't buy a new one. I'm not sure that school of thought is going to work on this old thing."

"I can give it a look," John told him. "If you want."

Tom Parker kept tugging and twisting things, still talking into the baler. "You looking for work?"

John quickly replied. "Yes, sir. Saw your sign."

"Can you ride?"

"Got my horse behind my truck. My own gear. I can ride, rope, wrangle—whatever you need. I know cattle. Maybe even fix that baler."

"Well, that would be a plus."

Tom pulled up to stand tall and turned around to look at him. John took in a silent breath while the elder Parker looked him over. "Well, shit," he said. "You're the Rankin boy. Been a while. How's your family?"

John straightened his shoulders and stood a little taller. He let that breath ease out between his lips. "Mom passed a few years ago," he told him. "Dad had a hard time of it after that. He closed the shop. He drinks too much and pretty much stares at the television."

"Sorry to hear that." Tom eyed him. "And you?"

"I've been working ranches in Idaho, Wyoming."

"I meant drinking."

Ah, now here it comes. "No sir. Not much since—"

"High school? When you and Tom and Cody got a little full of yourselves and ran my truck into the creek?"

John blew out the rest of that breath and his chest deflated. "Yes, sir. I apologize for that. I understand why you ordered me off the ranch. Can't say I've not had anything to drink since that night, but I will say I'm always responsible. I've grown up. Learned my lesson."

Tom Parker scooted away from the baler, looking back into the machine. "Yes, son. That's good. I wish Cody had learned that lesson."

The thought of Cody almost made John tear up. While John had decided to clean up his act, Cody had embraced drinking as a lifestyle and was now an alcoholic. He'd been in and out of jail too many times because of alcohol-related incidents. "Yes. I wish he had."

Tom didn't linger on that subject, and John was grateful. "So why are you back, John?"

There it was. The question. "It was time. Things weren't going well for me in Idaho—chalk that one up to a woman."

"Women can either be a blessing or a curse." Tom laughed.

John smiled. "Thought it would be good for my dad, too. Maybe I can get him up and out of that recliner and back into his garage and working. Or something. Tom said you might have work." *Probably good for me, too.*

"Never a bad idea to come back home, son."

"No, sir."

He stared into the guts of the baler. "Think you can fix this thing?"

"I can try. What's wrong with it?"

"Needs a good going over. We're baling here in a few weeks. We should have tackled this over the winter, but other things were priority then. Looks like a couple of welds are weak and something is going on with the knotter, for sure."

John nodded. "Let me look. I've worked on my share of ranch machinery and implements."

"Can you weld?"

"Yes, sir."

"Then you got a job." He tossed the wrench onto the workbench." I'm headed to the house for supper. You know where the bunkhouse is. Stash your gear there. Find and empty bunk and claim it. I've got three other wranglers staying there too. There's room for your horse in the barn and you can park your truck and trailer on the south side of the bunkhouse. I got three rules about my property: No fighting, no drinking, and clean up after yourself. If you can live by that, then we'll be good."

"Yes, sir. I can do that."

"Good." Tom stared him down for a moment. "Come to the house in a while and get something to eat. Annie will fix you a plate. You know your way to the kitchen, I assume. It's still in the same place."

John nodded. "Yes, sir. Thank you. I'll get right to work."

Tom wiped his hands on a shop towel and headed for the open barn door. Then, turning back, he stared John straight in the eyes. "And rule four—I made this one special for you, since you seem to have trouble with women. My daughter Annie? She's off limits. Got that?" His glare said as much as his words.

The warning shot up John's spine like a prick of adrenaline. "Yes, sir. Got it."

∽

"YOU HIRED JOHN RANKIN?"

Annie Parker didn't look at her father as she cleared the table and removed the food bowls and dishes to the counter. She wondered how her father would react to her question. He and her brother still sat at the table with their cups of coffee, as was their custom after dinner, discussing plans for the following day and the week. With a dry dish towel in hand, she moved to the tabled and wiped up crumbs while they sipped their brew.

"John stopped by?" Her brother sat up a little straighter and peered over his cup. "He called last week, and I told him you might have work. I forgot to mention it, Dad."

Annie watched the exchange between the two. Her dad ignored the question but glared directly at her. "How'd you know that?" His voice was gruff, but after eighteen years of living with him, she knew that gruffness was mostly smoke and mirrors with her. Now, the ranch hands didn't know that—so it was a different story for them—but she sure did.

"I talked to him earlier. Saw him heading up the road when I was coming in from checking the fences." Cupping one hand at the edge of the table, she caught the crumbs as she brushed them into her hand, then turned to toss them into the sink.

Annie would be glad when her mother was home from visiting her grandmother. She'd rather be out on the ranch working cattle than in the house cooking dinner. Leaning into the counter at the sink, she stared out the window over it. "Besides, his truck and trailer are parked over there by the bunkhouse, and I saw him put his horse in the barn before dinner."

"You always had an eagle eye."

Turning, she smiled. "You taught me to be aware of my surroundings."

His face turned stern. "Just don't you get too aware of John Rankin's surroundings, Annie. You hear me?"

Her brother scooted away from the table, the wooden chair screeching a bit on the plank floors. "Well good. I'm glad he made it. I'll check in with him."

"Wait until we're finished here. Let's include him in our work plans for this week. See how many more men we need to hire. We have hay to bale and cattle to move."

"That baler fixed?" Tom positioned his chair closer to the table again.

"John's working on it now." He turned to Annie. "Oh, by the way, fix him a plate while you're cleaning up. I told him to come by when he's finished and get dinner."

Annie nodded, smiling a little to herself as she turned back to the counter. "Sure thing, Dad. I can take it to him at the bunkhouse and leave it there for him."

Her father cleared his throat. "You'll do none of the sort, Annie Parker. Stay away from that bunkhouse. I told him to stop in. He'll stop in. Just get the plate ready."

Annie looked at her reflection in the kitchen window and smiled. "Yes, daddy."

After a minute, a rap sounded at the back door and John Rankin stepped inside the kitchen. The screen door slapped closed behind him. Annie snapped her attention toward him as he took off his hat and perched it on a peg by the door.

He glanced her way, tossing her a half grin, then jerked away to look at her father. "Just stopping in to pick up a plate."

"Come over here and sit a minute, John." Her dad motioned him toward the table.

John sidled another glance toward her.

Annie tossed him what she hoped was a shy, but sassy little smile—since her back was to her father and hopefully he couldn't see—then dropped her gaze to the food. "I'm working on that plate right now," she said. "Be ready in a minute."

"Yes, ma'am."

Annie turned and parked her fists on her hips. "Good heavens, John Rankin. Don't go ma'aming me. I'm at least ten years younger than you."

He halted. "Sorry. I…." He didn't finish the sentence. His eyes twinkled at her and her heart fluttered.

Tom Jr. rose, breaking the moment. "Hell. Get over here and have a seat, man. Been too long." He slapped John on the back and gave him a bear hug. Annie watched as the two sat, returning to her task of getting his plate ready. All the while, she watched his reflection in the kitchen window, recalling the nights when she was a silly young girl who practice-kissed her pillow every night, pretending she was kissing her older brother's best friend.

She'd had such a crush on him back then. Seemed seeing him earlier today had sparked some of those old emotions.

Today, she was sure kissing the man sitting at her kitchen table behind her would be a lot more interesting than kissing and hugging her pillow. She looked up and caught his gaze again in the window reflection. He grinned a little, and she smiled back.

Sigh.

Her father won't approve, of course. At least not at first.

But she had a way with her Daddy.

Smoke and mirrors, Annie. Smoke and mirrors.

Chapter One

May 1998, Twenty years later
Rankin's Rock Creek Ranch

JOHN RANKIN LOOKED DOWN ON THE FRESHLY COVERED gravesite, swiped his nose with the back of his hand, and wondered how in the hell he was going to raise two kids without their mother. He stared at the granules of Montana sand shifting over the grave and held the moment steady in his heart for as long as he could, because when he turned around and got into his truck where his children, Parker and Callie waited, and then headed back to the ranch, things were going to be different.

Painfully different.

Inhaling deep, he lifted his gaze to look out over the family burial plot and beyond. Situated high in the hills behind the ranch, this piece of land was the spot where Anne Parker Rankin's family rested. And where his wife, Anne, now rested too.

Annie. His beautiful Annie.

"Oh, Annie-girl, how am I going to do this without you?"

He was ten years her senior and became smitten the first day he laid eyes on her, when he'd returned to Montana. The ranch, known then as the Parker Ranch, was owned by Tom Parker, Sr., Annie's father. The old man had given him a rough row to hoe for a while—when he'd come looking for a job—but John had taken it and then some, because he figured he'd be lucky enough to sneak an occasional peek at the rancher's daughter if he stayed.

He'd fought for her love and had to prove to her father he was worthy. He'd married later than a lot of men his age, but when the sweet and young Annie entered his life, she hooked him with the power of her love—and her determination that he deserved to be loved by her.

She was nineteen when they married. He was twenty-nine. Their son, Parker, was born the next year. Callie took a little more time coming. He and the kids were her life, and she was theirs.

Annie loved him with all her heart, although he didn't know why. He could be a gruff, stubborn man, ignoring her for days on end while he tended to the ranch and the animals. Nothing he could help. It was their livelihood, and Annie understood that. In the early days, she'd worked right beside him. After the children came, she'd been content to see to home and hearth. And he'd never had to worry about her running around behind his back.

Life was wonderful.

Until she found the lump.

Tears stung his eyes as John peered down at the ranch house he'd built for her on the family land. Annie's grandparents had deeded them a section of the ranch when they married. Later, when her folks passed, the rest of the Parker land came to them.

That's when they changed the name of the ranch to

Rankin's Rock Creek Ranch—sometimes referred to as the Triple R. And that's when the ranch became his and he finally felt like he was at home and settled for the first time in his life.

After a life of heartache growing up, and a decade of working ranches from Wyoming to Idaho, he'd finally settled down and had never been happier. A ranch of his own, a beautiful wife who loved him, and a son and a daughter he adored.

How in the hell was he going to step one foot away from this grave, and another closer to the rest of his life? How was he going to go on without his Annie?

He didn't know.

Chapter Two

*S*eptember, four months later....

"I will not!"

Eleven-year-old Callie Rankin stood hands on hips in the center of the Rankin family kitchen and shouted at her father. John did a double-take, staring at his daughter and wondering what in hell was wrong with the girl. She had never in her life raised her voice to him. Not like this, anyway.

"Callie, you're not wearing that make-up to school. Go do what I said, now, and take it off."

"No!"

Dumbfounded, John shook his head again and took a step toward his daughter. He reached out to grasp her arm, but realized how angry he was and stopped himself. *Get a grip.* She's not one of your wranglers. She's just a little girl and you are the adult here.

The parent. Her father. *Act like it.*

He stepped away, turning his back, then strode over to the

sink and began rinsing dishes and putting them in the dishwasher. Where in the hell did she get make-up, anyway? He should probably make eye contact with her, but at this moment, he couldn't.

"Then you're staying home from school today."

"Great." Callie raced off for the sofa in the great room.

Hell, that wasn't the right approach, either.

"If she doesn't have to go, then you know I ain't going either."

John shoved another glass into the dishwasher, glad it was plastic, and looked at his sixteen-year-old son, Parker. "You are going to school today and so is she. Get your stuff together because we're heading down to meet the bus in five minutes." There would be no time for them to walk down the ranch road this morning to catch the bus. He'd have to drive them.

Parker rolled his eyes and retreated up the back stairwell. John heaved a sigh, hung his head a bit, and glanced into the great room. Callie sat there with her feet propped up on the coffee table, remote control in hand, scanning through channels. He dampened a clean dish towel under the faucet, squeezed out the excess water, and moved determinedly into the room. Taking the remote control out of her hand, he said, "Stand up."

"Hey!" She jumped to her feet. "Give me that."

John grasped her hand that was groping toward the remote control. "Callie, stop it right now." He did nothing but hold her arm, but she twisted and pulled so much that he let her go, fearing she'd fracture a bone if he didn't.

And then where would they be.

Callie burst back. "I hate you!"

"No, you don't, Callie." John blew out a breath.

"I do."

He expected her to run away but she didn't. She stood

right there in front of him, in defiance. He lowered his voice. "You don't hate me, Callie. You're just missing your mama."

Her face turned red and she started shaking. "Why do you think I wanted to wear Mommy's make-up?"

Ah, shit.

She melted into tears. John caught her up in his arms and held her against him. "I love you, baby girl. It's okay. I didn't realize about the make-up, and I know this isn't easy." He didn't even know any of Annie's makeup was still around. Callie must have confiscated it weeks ago.

He was exhausted. This was not the first meltdown since Annie had died. Probably wouldn't be the last. He'd be glad when school was out for fall break, although it seemed like school had just started—at least they would avoid the morning fight for a week.

"I...love you, Daddy." Called hiccupped a sob and John just held her. "Sorry."

"I know."

Parker bounded down the stairs and into the great room. John investigated his son's questioning face. "No one's going to school today. And I'm not working. We are all taking the day off."

THE NEXT DAY, JOHN PACED TEN FEET ONE WAY AND THEN THE other in the barn, raking his fingers over his short hair. The morning had gone a lot easier than yesterday—and the kids were off to school without incident—but something still agitated him about Callie and how to help her. His gut ached just thinking about it. He hated that she still hurt so much.

But hell. He still hurt from losing Annie. Why shouldn't he expect that she'd still be hurting too?

"I just don't know what to do with her, Buck."

Buck McGinnis, his ranch manager, chewed a piece of hay, one foot propped up on a bucket. "Kristin says Callie is having some trouble at school. Says she talked back to the teacher yesterday and had to go have a conversation with the principal."

"Yes. I got that call. We have a meeting with Principal Sloan and the school counselor on Friday."

"Maybe that will help at school."

"And I hope at home, too. I'm about at my wit's end."

Buck and his daughter, Kristin, had lived on the ranch for nearly a decade. They'd moved into the apartment over the bunkhouse after John asked Buck to oversee the work of the wranglers, freeing him up to focus on other aspects of the ranch. Buck soon became one of the best ranch managers around and a trusted friend. Kristin was Callie's age, which was nice for his daughter. John had been glad, especially lately, that the girls had each other growing up around all the boys and men on the ranch.

"What else does Kris say?"

Buck shook his head. "Not much. Just that Callie's still taking Anne's passing hard."

Nothing John didn't already know. "I thought I knew my girl, but she sure is pulling a switch on me."

Buck stood. "She's at that age, John. Kris pulls some drama queen acts on me from time to time. I think it's those hormones."

John jerked his head up to look at Buck. "Hell no. The girls are too young."

Buck shook his head. "Naw. They're not, John. Seriously. There is a lot going on with girls this age, or so I gather."

John stared at him. "How'd you get so smart?"

He shrugged. "I just ask questions. When Kris's mom left us, I got good at asking other women what to expect. Get their advice. I try to remember what they tell me."

John thought about that. "What do you think is going on with Callie?"

Buck didn't immediately answer. "John, I can't say for sure. Maybe you need to talk to someone other than school personnel. Maybe she needs some outside counseling. Someone to talk with about dealing with her mom passing and not being here for her as a woman. You know? I guess what I am saying is, maybe you could get some professional advice."

Professional help? That thought struck John in the heart like a dagger. *No. No.* "I don't think so, Buck."

Buck exhaled. "Well then, maybe you need to go out and find you a woman to talk to. Maybe even more than talk if you know what I mean. And if you don't know where to find one, just let me know."

John snorted and balked at that. "The last damn thing I need, Buck, is a woman."

Buck snagged John's eye. "Maybe it's not just you, John. Maybe Callie needs a woman to talk to about girl things."

Breaking Buck's stare, John glanced away and rubbed at a tightness that suddenly gripped his chest. "I can do fine by Callie. I'm not about to go about trying to find a woman to replace her Mom. That's not the answer here."

Standing up straight, Buck hitched up his Wranglers. "Not saying you need to find a wife, John. Or a mother for Callie. But perhaps you both could use some feminine influence in your lives."

John stared at the barn floor.

"What's it been, John, a few months since Anne passed? I mean no disrespect, and I also know that's not been an awfully long time, but maybe some occasional companionship with someone soft and willing would cure what ails you, too."

John jerked up his head and glared. "Shit, Buck. I don't have ails."

"The hell you don't. And it's okay if you need a temporary reprieve from the daily grind around here."

"We're talking about Callie, not me."

"Could be one and the same."

Staring at his friend, John cocked his head to the side. "What are you saying?"

"You're still grieving, John. And that's okay. But it's also okay to give yourself a time-out occasionally and get away from the ranch, and even your family. For your health and sanity. The kids see how hard this is on you, and you can't keep up the pace you've set for yourself and raise your family too. I'm not saying you need to fall in love. I'm just saying that some casual adult time—whatever that turns out to be—couldn't hurt."

Adult time. Hell. That was something he'd not had in an awfully long time. Not since before Annie got sick. He wasn't sure he could do it. "Seems far-fetched to help Callie."

"You have to help yourself first, John, before you can help your girl. I can set you up with a date if you want. Just say the word."

"Not sure the kind of women you hang with will be much help with a little girl."

Buck chuckled and shrugged. "I'm not talking buckle bunnies or barflies—although if that's what you're in the market for, I can hook you up there, too. It might surprise you that I know a few people who don't hang around in saloons or at the rodeo." He laughed, turning toward a stall. Reaching into his pocket for a quarter apple, he fed it to the Palomino stalled there. "I actually know a couple of women—one in particular—who might be interested in conversating with the rancher John Rankin."

"That's what scares me most."

Laughing, Buck stroked the horse's muzzle. "Nothing you can't handle." He stopped, catching John's eye again. "But hell,

John, you have to do something. If not for you, then for Callie. Just let me know and I'll make the call. Her name's Abby Cooper and she works at the library over in Livingston."

John raised a brow. "You know a librarian?"

Buck pushed away from the stall, chuckling. "I do read." Heading down the center aisle of the barn, he added, "Kris is a bookworm. Her library card has saved me a hell of a lot of money the past couple of years. Not ashamed to say I've checked out a few myself."

"Well, I'll be damned."

Buck stopped and turned back. "We go every Saturday, so I'm heading over there tomorrow. Let me test the waters and I'll get back to you."

Shit. John nodded. "Fine."

"Great."

"I'm not saying yes. I'm just saying fine."

"Whatever you say, boss."

Buck whistled as he swaggered through the barn and out the door. John wondered just what he had agreed—or didn't agree—to. Either way, seemed Buck had set out on some sort of damn mission.

Chapter Three

"I'd like you to meet someone, Abby."

Abby Cooper looked up from the stack of books she'd just pulled from the return bin in the library desk and blinked. The words exiting Buck McGinnis' mouth were not what she expected to hear. He'd asked her out so many times it was getting annoyingly redundant—but this time he'd thrown her a curve ball.

"Excuse me?"

Buck stood looking at her, fiddling with his cowboy hat in his hands. He glanced to his left, where his daughter explored the stacks of young adult fiction, then back to her. "I know you told me you don't date," he whispered, then curled his mouth into a grin. "At least you said you wouldn't date me. But I was wondering if you'd meet a friend of mine."

What in the world? Abby picked up the stack of five books and added them to the nearly full library cart. "You know why I said I wouldn't date you. Right?" She looked at him straight on.

The cowboy standing in front of her cleared his throat.

"Yes, ma'am. I still have too much rodeo in my blood, and you want nothing to do with rodeo after your ex cheated on you."

Abby huffed. "Don't you mean serial cheated with a string of *rode-hard-and-put-up-wet* barrel racers?"

Cocking his head to the side, Buck grinned. "Well, since you put it that way, I can see why you're not too keen on rodeo."

Nodding, Abby said, "Exactly."

Buck studied her. "So, if you won't date me, perhaps you'd meet a friend of mine? I think he could use some female companionship."

Abby felt her right eyebrow spike into an arch. It was an uncontrollable and instant reaction. She squared her shoulders and gripped the handles of the library cart. Leaning in, she used her best firm-but-quiet librarian voice, hoping to let him know in no uncertain terms what she thought of his request. "Buck McGinnis, I'm not one of those two-bit buckle bunnies or washed-up barrel racer cowgirls you keep company with on your free weekends. So no, I'm not available to be your friend's *female companionship*."

"Ah shit, Abby."

"Watch your language and lower your tone."

He stared. "I didn't mean it like that. First, I'm a little old for chasing fillies. Gave that up a few years ago. And second, John Rankin doesn't even go to rodeo anymore. Hasn't for years. Especially lately. He's been too busy with his kids and the ranch since his wife died. I just thought the two of you might hit it off. Never mind." He turned and glanced at Kris. "Forget I said anything."

Abby didn't say another word. She watched him stroll off to where Kris stood pulling books off the shelf and reading the back copy blurbs. Pushing the library cart full of books, she followed him.

Kris moved down the stacks. Abby sidled up next to Buck. "It would never work," she whispered, leaning toward him.

Buck faced her. "Why? You don't know him. Do you?"

She shook her head. "No. But I know of him. Everyone knows the Rankins or has heard of them. And his wife hasn't been gone that long. I will not be his rebound girlfriend. Besides, it's too soon for him."

"Maybe it's too soon for you." His stare into her eyes intensified.

"Has nothing to do with me, Buck. My divorce has been over for years. But I do have Luke to consider."

Buck rubbed the stubble of his chin. "That's right. You have the boy."

She nodded. "Yes, and he is getting into that influential age, you know? Of course, he loves rodeo, just like his dad, and I'm not sure I'll ever get that out of him."

"So maybe he needs another influence. Another man in his life. Ranching is hard, respectable, work and a good substitute for rodeo, or has been in my experience."

"I see how that's worked out for you so well." She grinned.

A corner of Buck's mouth jerked up, along with his mustache. "I'm too old for competition, unless it's an occasional charity event or something—but I still like to watch. I get enough exercise wrangling calves and breaking bucks in my day-to-day life these days on the ranch. It's decent work and satisfies me."

Abby pretended to examine the book in her hand, eyeballing the numbers on the spine. She shoved it into a spot on the shelf with the rest of the young adult books, promising that later she'd come back and make sure she had shelved it properly.

Facing him, she said, "Now you're taking another tack, Buck McGinnis. I doubt John Rankin needs another child in his life to mentor. Sounds like he has his hands full."

"Maybe you're right." He glanced off toward Kris again, then faced her. "But honestly, I think John needs a friend more than a girlfriend."

"Doesn't he have you?"

Buck nodded. "Yes. Of course. But I think he needs a woman—"

Abby shot him a look.

"Not in that way." He stepped closer. "What I mean is, well, he has a daughter. She's Kris's age. And she's going through those years. I thought maybe…."

Backing off, Abby put up her hands. "No, Buck. I get where you are going with this but I… I can't." She glanced at the big clock above the library desk. It was near lunchtime, and she could use that as her exit. "Look. If I'm ever going to date again, it's going to be for me. Not for my son or his daughter. That will never work."

"But maybe it could start off that way?"

She shook her head. "No." Glancing at her watch, she added, "It's time for my lunch break. I'll see you next weekend." Abby looked down the stack to Kris and noticed the girl's arms were full of books. "Or whenever Kris finishes reading those. Have a good weekend, Buck."

With that, she left the cart of books in the stacks, nodded to Mrs. Peterson behind the desk, who volunteered during lunch breaks, and hurried out the back door of the library to her car.

AFTER GRABBING A SANDWICH AT A FAST-FOOD PLACE—BECAUSE she'd left so quickly she forgot to pick up her tuna salad in the library refrigerator before she left—Abby drove to Sacajawea Park in Livingston. The park was a few blocks away, and the drive took several minutes, but was worth it. Finding a quiet spot, she pulled over and parked where she could see the river.

She sat there for a while mesmerized by the flow of the Yellowstone, and immersed herself in the calming effects of the Absaroka Mountains in the distance.

What Buck had asked of her wasn't so bad, really. Was it? And she was right in saying that her divorce was over years ago and it wasn't a factor in her decision to meet John Rankin. And Luke? He was only twelve, but she was seeing signs of his father in him, even at his young age. She should expect that. Luke visited with his father every other weekend and in the summers, traveled with him for a few weeks while his dad was on tour. She hated thinking about how all that influenced him, but she couldn't keep Luke away from his dad—he had visitation rights—and subsequently, she couldn't ban him from rodeo either.

It wasn't that Branden Cooper was a bad man. He just liked women a little too much.

She supposed with Luke, what would be, would be. Perhaps it was up to her to teach him how to treat and love a woman the right way.

And how am I going to do that? Teach by example? Which means I need to let my insecurities go and meet someone—or risk affecting Luke's future by leaving it to fate. Can I do that? All Luke knows is how Brand treats me. And that's not so great, still to this day, even when they meet casually.

Exhaling deep, Abby's shoulders relaxed a little, and she glanced at the unopened fast-food bag on her passenger seat. She should eat that before her lunch got cold.

Maybe Buck was right. Maybe Luke needed a different male role model, other than his father. And maybe she could use a little male companionship, too.

Tearing into the bag and unwrapping her sandwich, she took a bite of her hamburger and chewed over those thoughts. Absentmindedly, she picked through her fries, then crumbled up the half-eaten bag and stuffed it back into the fast-foot sack. The rest of her uneaten hamburger followed.

She watched the water rush by for a few more minutes. Moving swiftly today, it reminded her of how fast life, time, moved. Lately, each day sped by at a clippety-clop pace. Before long, she'd be thirty-five years old and pushing forty. Luke would be a teenager doing his own thing and she'd still be stuck in the library shelving books.

Not that she didn't love her job. She did. But what would she do with her life once Luke was grown and out of the house? That day was going to come, and quickly.

Did she need more in her life than her job and Luke? For years she hadn't thought she did. Now, she wasn't so sure.

Abby shook herself and started the car. "Not going to solve this problem today," she said aloud. "And meeting John Rankin likely isn't going to solve it, either."

Or would it?

What could it hurt? She had to start putting herself out there at some point. Right?

THAT NEXT SATURDAY MORNING, A WEEK LATER, ABBY WAS ready when Buck stepped back through the library doors. He followed Kris, who entered with the same stack of books in her arms that she left with last week.

The girl plopped all the books on the counter and grinned at Abby.

"You read all these this week?"

Still grinning, Kris's words tumbled out. "Yes! I loved this new teenage witch series and I read every one of them back-to-back. I can't wait for the next one to come out."

Abby glanced at Buck and pulled the books toward her to check them in. "You stay up all night?"

Kris grinned. "Not all night." She looked at her dad.

"Good thing, since you have school the next day. Right?" Buck nudged his daughter's arm.

Kris shrugged and grinned.

Abby opened a book. "Well, I'm sure your teacher is pleased with the number of books you are reading this year. Are you keeping a log?"

"Yep. I have them all in a notebook."

"Good."

Kris beamed.

Abby continued. "You know, I've heard the author of that teenage witch series is coming out with the next installment around Halloween."

Kris's face lit up and she glanced at her dad. "That's close to my birthday! Maybe I can get the next one for my very own as a birthday gift. What do you think, Dad?"

Abby watched Buck smile affectionately at his daughter. "Oh, I suppose we could spare a few dollars for a book of very your own—for a birthday present, you know."

"Of course!"

Abby grinned and looked at Buck. "You know, they say the more books in the home, the better prepared the child for school and beyond. Of course, checking books out of the library is important too—and Kris sure does her share of doing that and actually reading the books—but a home library is also important."

Nodding, Buck looked again at Kris. "You make a list, girl. Let's see what we can do. But we're still checking out books here every week."

Kris beamed. "Thanks, Dad!"

Abby watched her scoot off toward the stacks. "She's a good kid, Buck. And smart. You've done well."

He laughed. "I'm sure she gets a few of those smarts from her mama, although I can't say for sure."

That made Abby curious. "Why?"

"Well, we—Kris and I—haven't seen her for years. Not sure where she is."

"Oh, I'm sorry, Buck. I didn't know that."

He shrugged. "It's okay. We fell in love quickly. The baby came too quickly, to be sure. We weren't ready. She just couldn't handle it all."

"She left?"

Buck nodded. "One morning I got up to a note on the kitchen table telling me not to look for her. Kris was eighteen-months-old."

"Did you?"

"What?"

"Look for her."

He lowered his gaze. "No, I didn't. I'd always thought I might, but life got overwhelming for a while. Too many years have passed now."

Abby gently nodded in agreement. "I understand, Buck." She reached out and touched his arm.

His gaze met hers. "You see, I've been overwhelmed with life too. Like John. Not trying to beat a dead horse here, Abby. It's just that I see John like that right now. He sure helped me out when I was at my lowest. Gave me a job, and Kris and me a home. Not sure I can ever repay him for that. But all I was thinking was maybe the two of you could meet up for dinner sometime. Just a bit of a getaway in this hectic world we live in."

Abby started to speak but Buck put up his hand. "You know, sometimes you have to be good to yourself so you can be good for others."

"I'm not denying that. Okay, Buck." Abby let go of a pent-up breath.

"Now, I know what you said and I'm not here today to talk you into it, Abby. I'm just explaining why—"

"I'll meet him," Abby interrupted.

"What?"

"I'll have dinner with John Rankin. But that's all it is. Dinner."

"Of course, Abby. You're sure?"

She nodded. "Yes, I am. I need to figure some things out too, and the only way I can do that is jump into the fire, I guess. Besides, I could use a change of pace myself."

Buck gave her a knowing grin. "When are you free?"

Abby thought about that. "Luke comes home tomorrow from his weekend with his dad. I'd like to mull this over just a bit to get myself prepared. How about in two weeks? Luke will be back with his dad then. Will that weekend work?"

"I'm sure it will, Abby. Now, I just need to get with John."

"Does he know what you are doing?"

"Naw. Well, sort of. I've brought it up and he's reluctant, but I'm cracking away at him."

"You're going to need those two weeks for the reluctant rancher," Abby said.

Buck chuckled. "I think you are probably right. I'll be in touch." He glanced off. "Now, point me toward those western books you were talking about a while back."

Abby smiled. "Louis L'Amour? Right this way."

Chapter Four

*J*ohn took one last look at himself in the mirror, exited his bedroom, and hesitantly descended the stairwell. Unsure of himself, he landed in the great room and spied his children sprawled on the couch watching a movie. Their gazes simultaneously slid his way. Callie's mouth dropped open. Parker stared.

"Good movie?" he asked, trying to break the awkward mood—wondering if his kids sensed it too.

They ignored him.

"Thought you were going to a meeting?" Parker finally spoke.

John strolled determinedly into the room. "I am." *Sort of.*

Callie scooted to the edge of the couch. "Those aren't meeting clothes, Dad. Those are going out to dinner clothes. And you smell."

Cocking a brow at his daughter, John said, "Smell?"

"Yeah, like man perfume."

Great. I overdid it with the aftershave. Dammit. What the hell am I doing here?

John ignored her and lowered his gaze, avoiding making

eye contact with the kids while he strolled past the sofa. "It's a dinner meeting in Bozeman," he mumbled. "Cattlemen's association. I need to get a move on." He turned to look at Callie. "And for your information, these are meeting clothes and I think I smell real purty."

He chuckled, hoping to get a laugh or something out of her, but her expression remained deadpan.

Parker stood. "I thought that was in Vaughn. Next week."

"What?"

"The Cattlemen's Association. You usually meet in Vaughn. Right?"

Clearing his throat, John glared at his son. "Right. But we're meeting in Bozeman tonight. It's a...committee meeting." He cleared his throat. "Now, you two stay put and behave. Buck and Kris will be here soon with pizza."

"Oh good!" Callie plopped back on the couch and returned to the movie.

Parker eyed his father.

"I'm heading out now." John dodged Parker's glare. "Watch your sister."

"Have fun."

He moved toward the back door and grasped his hat from a peg on the wall. "These meetings usually aren't fun, son."

Parker didn't miss a beat. "Like I said, have fun."

John turned and made direct eye contact with his son, who stood before him stone-still, a blank expression on his face. "I'll try."

Parker cracked a slight grin then. "Callie and I will be fine. Be safe."

"Always."

Leaving the house, John wondered what Parker knew, or thought he knew. He hadn't wanted the kids to know what he was doing tonight. He didn't like being dishonest, but tonight was not the night to let them know he was meeting a woman, no matter how casual. It was none of their business and children do not need to know everything.

No need to tell them he had a date. *Sort of.* No, not a date.

But dinner sounded like a date, didn't it? At least he wasn't picking her up at her home. They had agreed, through Buck, to meet at the Open Range restaurant in Bozeman. He hadn't spoken with her yet.

Stopping short of his truck, he stared out over the ranch. Should he have called her sometime this week just to chat and get the opening night jitters out of the way? *Shit.* He didn't know what in the hell he was doing here. What did people do these days when dating? Times were different nearly twenty years ago when he and Annie got together.

He was too old to start this dating game at this point in his life.

Hell, was he doing the right thing? Meeting her?

Probably not.

And why was he doing it anyway? Just to get Buck off his back? To get out of the house for a few hours?

Or because he was lonely?

Annie-girl, forgive me.

ABBY LET THE SCREEN DOOR TO HER HOUSE SWING CLOSED behind her with a slap. She jumped, unsure when she'd been so nervous. Her stomach churned with anticipation, and she wondered if she could truly do this. She'd not been out to dinner with a man other than Brand in years. She had to stop thinking about this as a date. It wasn't. She'd made that perfectly clear to Buck. This was just a meet-up to see if they were compatible, or liked each other, or something. That felt awfully stiff and impersonal, in a way, but safer for her mental state if she kept that notion in her head.

Not a date, Abby.

It still feels like a date.

At least she was driving herself to the steakhouse. She had her getaway vehicle. That helped her feel secure. And if things went terribly bad, she could always excuse herself to the restroom and duck out the back door of the restaurant to make her escape.

Great, Abby. Quit thinking about escaping before you meet him.

She got in her Chevy SUV and headed toward Bozeman, glad for the twenty-five-mile drive from where she lived in Livingston. The miles of quiet should help clear her head a little.

At least they were meeting in the bar. They had decided on drinks first, at Buck's suggestion. If things went well from there, then perhaps dinner. If not, she could always excuse herself after a glass of wine.

Stop it, Abby. Stop thinking about leaving!

But she needed a plan. That made her feel better, at least. Her brain rolled over various scenarios the entire ride into the city—and how she would handle them.

If he wanted to buy her dinner, but she was ready to go, she'd make an excuse to get home. Perhaps to catch her goodnight call from Luke. That could work.

If he suggested they go somewhere else, she could do the same.

What if he suggested they go back to her place? Panic skipped down her spine. She'd not had a man in her house for any length of time since Brand left. Do people do that these days? Go back to one of their places after drinks or dinner? She didn't know the dating protocol anymore. What was expected of her?

What did *he* expect? A quickie hook-up?

Oh, hell.

She was not ready for that.

Or was she?

Goodness, Abby. You are a mess.

"Quit letting your mind wander and focus on the one scenario that is likely to happen. Meet him, have a drink, share some conversation, go home. End of night."

Before she knew it, she was in Bozeman and pulling into the parking lot of the steakhouse—early. She contemplated sitting there until she saw John Rankin go in, give him a minute or two to get settled, and then follow him inside. But she grew anxious waiting and finally, impulsively, threw her car door open, along with any caution she possessed, and headed toward the front door of the restaurant.

She needed a drink. Something stronger than wine. Bourbon. Maybe she could guzzle one down before the reluctant rancher arrived.

JOHN STAYED IN HIS TRUCK WHEN HE GOT TO OPEN RANGE. He'd backed in between two other vehicles and sat there in the far corner watching, wondering, whether this Abby Cooper would show up.

What kind of woman meets a man she doesn't know in a bar?

Hell, it wasn't her idea, so he couldn't blame her. It was Buck's. Right?

He supposed meeting in a bar wasn't such a bad idea. Besides, the bar at Open Range was rather upscale. It was public. Lots of people around. Not so intimate. A convenient place to have a drink and share some conversation, and perhaps determine if there was any compatibility between the two of them.

And if not, well, the night would end.

Then this thing would be done, Buck would be satisfied, and he could get back home where he belonged with his kids.

He had half a mind to leave and forget the whole thing. What would it matter? He didn't know her. She didn't know him. All they knew of each other was through Buck. He could pull out of here right now and forget the whole damn thing. Better for the two of them. He had no business starting something he couldn't finish.

Because he couldn't picture himself with anyone but his wife. What the hell was he doing?

Keys still in the ignition, he was about to twist them and start his truck when he saw her.

A flash caught his eye as the setting sun reflected off a door mirror down the way and a tall woman stepped from between the parked vehicles and moved toward the front of the restaurant. He watched as she strode across the lot and instinctively, he knew the woman was Abby Cooper. She was just as Buck had described. Tall and thin, long auburn hair. "She moves with the grace of thoroughbred filly," Buck had said to him. He watched this woman glide inside the door, her head held high and her back straight, and knew for certain she was his date.

Dinner companion.

Whatever.

He didn't really know anything about her. He supposed that's what this night was for.

Suddenly, he was more intrigued than apprehensive.

Exiting the truck, he followed her across the parking lot.

Chapter Five

*A*bby stepped inside the restaurant, paused a moment to let her eyes adjust to the dim atmosphere, and glanced about the lobby. She'd never been here before, so wanted to gather her bearings. A young woman stood behind a desk area to her left.

"Good evening," the host said. "One for dinner? Or are you waiting for someone?"

"I'm meeting someone," Abby acknowledged. "He could be in the bar."

"Could be." The young woman pointed. "The bar is off to side there. Looks like there are plenty of seats for waiting. Should I put you on the dinner list?"

Abby smiled. "Um, I'm not certain. We will let you know."

"Of course."

Heading into the bar area, Abby soaked up the cozy western ambiance. Cream and yellow-gold tones and deep brown woods offered a subdued, soft ambiance against the warmth of brick and timber beams. She felt comfortable here so far, stepping up to the bar. Hopefully, the evening would progress with the same level of comfort.

She chose a seat. The bartender glanced her way. "An Old Fashioned," she told him. "With Woodford Reserve, if you have it."

Nodding, he returned, "Of course. Coming up."

Settling onto her seat, she glanced about, her gaze swinging to her left, and that's when she saw the tall, older cowboy making his entrance.

An impressive entrance.

This cowboy looked to be in his mid-forties. That would be the right age for John Rankin. He had a teenage son, according to Buck, who also told her that John's wife had been several years younger than him. The man was stocky, yet fit, with lean, but muscular, wrangler legs. Legs that had worked a lot of years on a ranch, on horseback. His jeans were new and starched, his boots pointed and polished, but well broken-in. He wore a white collared shirt beneath a brown sports coat that strangely complemented the warmth of the atmosphere in the bar. His belt sported a silver western buckle, but not a rodeo buckle. Thank the Lord. He carried his hat as he drew even with her chair.

"Excuse me. Abby?" The hat shook in his hand.

"Yes. Are you John?"

He nodded. "I am. Mind if I join you?"

She gave into a smile. "That's why we're here. Right?"

He let go of a breath then, chuckling. "Yes, ma'am." He sat, taking the seat at the bar beside of her, and positioned his hat back on his head. "I don't mind telling you, I'm a tad nervous."

Abby felt compassion for him at that moment. Before she realized it, she had reached out and laid her hand on the back of his forearm. "I don't mind telling you I'm nervous as hell."

John grinned.

The bartender placed her Old Fashioned in front of her. He glanced at John. "Sir?"

"A shot of Yellowstone."

"Coming up."

Abby watched John eye her drink. "Bourbon?" he asked

She removed her hand from his arm, grasped the tumbler, and took a quick sip. "Yes. I felt the occasion warranted something a little harder than wine." She set the glass down on the bar. "I see you're a bourbon whiskey fellow, too."

"Of course."

The bartender set his drink in front of him. John picked up the shot glass and quickly downed the bourbon. "Bring another one. On the rocks this time."

"Yes, sir."

Abby watched the tension in John's face relax a bit. "The Yellowstone brand is a good one," she said. "Interesting that it's made in Kentucky, but people often associate it with Montana and the park and all. There's a whole story about the origins of the distillery, but I've forgotten it."

"True. But in my opinion," John said, fiddling with his shot glass, "the best bourbon whiskeys come from Kentucky. What are you drinking there?"

"Woodford Reserve."

He nodded. "I've heard of it. It's relatively new. Isn't it?"

"Yes. It's been out a couple of years, I believe. A friend of mine in Kentucky introduced me to it a while back. Smooth, sweet, and woodsy. It's double-oaked. A good sipping whiskey, they say. You should try it sometime."

He eyed her then. "How do you know so much about whiskey?"

"Bourbon." Abby shrugged. "I went to college in Kentucky. You learn about such things when you live there."

"Ah, I see." He drummed his fingertips on the bar top and glanced away for a moment, then back again. "Buck tells me you are a librarian. Sorry to say I don't read many books."

"You know, I hear that a lot."

"From your other dates?"

She shook her head. "No. I don't really date."

"Ah, I see. Me, neither."

"Just from people I meet casually, or in the library."

"I see. I bet you do."

"I won't hold it against you." Abby watched John's face break into a smile.

"About not reading or not dating?"

Abby sipped her drink and then let out a little laugh. "Reading. I think this conversation has suddenly gone a little convoluted."

John nodded. "Like I said. I'm nervous."

"I'm the same. So, we're even."

The bartender interrupted again, setting John's drink in front of him. "Should I add you to the dinner list, sir?"

John shot her a glance. She gave him a slight, uncertain shrug. Their gazes connected and held. "Let's hold on that for a few minutes," he said to the bartender. But his stare remained, holding her captive.

Abby felt a bit of a warm tingle run down her spine, a sensation she hadn't felt in some time. It could have been the bourbon. Then again, it could be John Rankin's mesmerizing brown eyes—eyes that for some reason she felt she could look into for a long time.

After a moment, he pulled back and switched gears. "Have you been here before?" he queried. "Open Range, I mean."

She shook her head. "No. I don't get to Bozeman often," she told him. "Luke and I hang out in Livingston most of the time. I'm a bit of a homebody and I'm usually tired after work, so we often stay in."

John cocked a brow. "Luke?"

"Oh, my son. He's twelve going on forty-two."

Laughing, John said, "I see."

"I should have mentioned him before now."

"No reason to. We're just getting started. Where is Luke tonight?"

"He's with his dad. We've been divorced a few years now. It's his weekend."

"Ah. I see. My two—Callie and Parker—are home with Buck and his daughter, Kris. Of course, you know them. Callie is eleven. Her birthday is coming up this fall. Parker is sixteen. My wife…" He paused, looking away for a moment. "Well, she's been gone for several months now."

Abby nodded. "I know." She stared into her drink. "I'm sorry, John."

"Thank you."

An awkward pause settled between them. Abby took another reinforcing sip of her Old Fashioned and John threw back his whiskey. The ice in his tumbler clinked when he set the glass back on the bar.

"Bozeman has a lot of nice restaurants." John turned fully toward her on the bar stool. "Surely you go out to eat?"

Abby stared. "Actually, no. I don't date, John, as I said. I haven't for a while. Not since—" She really didn't want to go there. You aren't supposed to talk about your divorce or your ex on a first date with a new guy, are you? She'd read that somewhere. "And I rarely eat expensive steak," she blurted out.

That was stupid, Abby.

John stared at her for a few seconds, causing her to lower her gaze uncomfortably.

"You have something against steak?"

She grinned, looking up at him. "Not at all, Mr. Rancher. It's just not a priority on my salary with a twelve-year-old boy who eats like a horse."

"Are you comfortable here?" he blurted out.

"Oh, I'm comfortable. I'm just…."

"Anxious?"

"Somewhat. You?"

"Like a whore in church."

Abby laughed aloud.

"You want to get out of here?"

Studying him for a few seconds, Abby made a quick decision. "Yes. I think I do."

John nodded. "Me, too."

"Maybe someplace quiet would be more conducive to conversation." She eyed him, trying to gauge his reaction. "That is, if you prefer."

"I like the sound of that."

"Okay." Abby hesitated. Should she act on the thought in her head, or quickly try to think of something else?

"Got any ideas?"

She paused for a couple of heartbeats, then jumped in with both feet. Now or never. "I do. And if you are not okay with this idea, that's fine. We can come up with something else. But perhaps you can follow me back to Livingston? What about pizza and beer at my place? Or, whiskey, if you prefer. There's a new oven-fired pizza restaurant around the corner. We could pick one up or have it delivered."

John Rankin stood then, keeping eye contact with her. "Perfect."

"All right."

He pulled several bills out of his wallet, tossed them on the bar, and reached for her elbow. Abby stood and pulled her purse over her shoulder.

Leaning in as they stepped away from the bar, John whispered, "I like your style, Abby Cooper. And I'm following your lead."

Chapter Six

*I*n the wee hours of the next morning, John drove in silence toward home. Every mile took him farther away from Livingston—and Abby—and with each passing minute, he ticked off all the reasons why the last eight hours had been an extremely bad idea.

On one hand, he'd known Buck was right. Time away from the ranch and the kids was a probably a good idea. Why wouldn't an occasional adult evening spent in the company of a smart, beautiful, and classy woman be okay? He was well past the age of having to answer to anyone for his actions. He was no longer married, and Annie, God rest her soul, had even told him to find a woman after she passed. She didn't want him to be alone.

Not that he wanted any woman to move into his life and onto the ranch. He could never see that happening. But an evening out occasionally wasn't a terrible thing.

Was it?

But what if it turned into more? That's when things could turn sticky. Callie was a handful now, still missing her mama something awful. What would she do if another woman came into the picture?

And what about Parker? At sixteen, was his solemn moodiness normal, or was more working on him, too? What would his son think if there was a woman in his old man's life?

Not a good idea. Any woman he dated… Well, he'd have to be discreet and keep any knowledge of her to himself.

But that felt wrong.

Staring ahead through the windshield, he watched the sun peek up over the horizon with water-color strokes of orange, pink, and yellow bursting from the brown-green earth.

He'd stayed later than he had intended. He told her—told this Abby Cooper—that he needed to get back to the ranch. And of course, he did. He'd hoped like hell he could sneak in before the kids woke. Since it was the weekend, he counted on them sleeping in. Anyone else he could handle.

His mind drifted.

Abby Cooper.

He found it odd that he'd never seen her around. He knew a lot of people in Livingston. Turned out she lived on the far side of town from where his ranch sat, thirty miles away. Of course, John didn't frequent the library, so why would he have met her prior to last night?

But good ol' Buck—he'd come to the rescue. Or something.

Abby was beautiful, bright, and divorced. She seemed comfortable enough having a drink with him at the restaurant bar in Bozeman. She was even more comfortable later that evening as they shared a takeout pizza and beer in her living room—their boots kicked off and feet propped up on the coffee table, while watching a movie. They'd had an enjoyable time, talking and sharing into the early morning hours. In so many ways, he'd needed that adult conversation. And she confessed she did too.

He was drawn to her at once. Figuring out why, might take a little longer to digest.

Still, he enjoyed her company and told her so. She'd said the same.

So, when he'd made his move to say goodnight and she'd countered with a sweet kiss on his lips and asked him to stay, he couldn't say he was surprised.

What surprised him, was when he said he would.

John blinked several times and pushed the last few hours out of his head. His brain quieted and his thoughts stilled for several minutes as he rolled on. By the time he pulled onto the dirt road at Rock Creek Ranch, he was ready to get on with the day. Then, like a bolt of lightning, Abby's face burst into his mind's eye.

Quarreling emotions of guilt and pleasure rippled through his torso as he remembered her soft features, velvet skin, her open eyes gazing into his. He'd not been with another woman since he'd met Anne, and they'd been together for two decades. His need to bore deep into Abby and satisfy his physical urges conflicted with the remorse hammering at his heart.

But that hadn't stopped him from making love to Abby with all the tenderness and passion he wanted to give her. Needed to give her.

Her soft tears afterward were his undoing.

"Dammit." John pounded the steering wheel. Where did this leave him now?

Them?

The leaving had been awkward.

She'd slept curled against him, and he'd woke with the scent of her shampoo in his nostrils. Immediately, he'd felt a deep sense of guilt. Had he cheated on Annie? Had he started something with Abby he couldn't finish? That wasn't fair to her. Was it?

He wasn't sure if he liked another woman's scent in his nose upon waking.

You sure as hell didn't think this through, old man.

Abby had roused without a word or a backward glance, slipping out of bed and pulling the sheet with her. She tucked it around her body as she padded off to the bathroom. He dressed quickly while she was in there, ready to bolt, but waited. When she'd come out a few minutes later, tying her robe around her soft body, they both found it difficult to make eye contact.

He'd approached and given her a quick kiss on the forehead, mumbling a few words about needing to go, and that he'd had a nice time. She nodded, and he didn't look back as he left her place, without the promise of anything more to come.

A kiss on the forehead. He felt like a damned heel.

Pulling up to his house now, his gaze settled on the black diesel pickup truck parked off to the side. He sat for a minute, pondering why his brother-in-law was here before six o'clock in the morning. His shoulders slumped in semi-defeat.

"Shit." The word whistled through his teeth. "What the hell are you doing here, Tom Parker?"

"About time you showed your face this morning, old man. We were beginning to worry about you."

John exhaled and pushed through the back door. He did a quick assessment of the kitchen to figure out if he needed to be on the defensive. Only one person there that he could see, anyway.

"Mornin' Tom." He nodded to his brother-in-law, hung his coat on a peg by the back door, and his hat on the one next to it. "What in the world are you doing here?" He glanced at the stove. "And cooking breakfast, no less."

A woman's voice called out from the pantry. "Oh, hell, John. You know, Tom. He got a wild hair last night and we drove up for a visit." Tom's wife, Sally, bustled out of the adjoining pantry with a bag of flour and a carton of baking powder. She sidled up next to John and leaned up for a quick kiss on the cheek. "Don't be mad," she added, "you ought to know by now he never calls first."

He knew that. Annie's brother, Tom, carved his own way in life. Made his own rules. Most of the people around here did that, although Tom was a man not to be reckoned with. The Parker men rivaled the Rankins in stubbornness. There were times John wondered how Anne and Sally had put up with them all these years.

Sally sat the products down on the kitchen island. "By the way, we sent Buck home last night. Kris stayed the night with Callie."

He nodded. "That's fine. I'm sure Buck was glad for an evening to himself. Thanks." John pulled out a chair and sat. "And of course, I'm not mad. Surprised, though. Everything okay?"

Tom's ranch was a couple of hours due east, near Billings. The Parker family had originally owned two large tracts of Montana land. When Annie and Tom's parents were killed in a car accident fifteen years ago, Tom ended up with the Billings area ranch, and Annie inherited the western tract, near Yellowstone, now Rock Creek Ranch. Their younger brother, Noah—the wanderer of the family, who worked ranches from Canada to Texas—had no desire to be tethered to a piece of land and was happy enough to inherit cash. They'd not seen Noah for several years—although he called or dropped a postcard occasionally—until Annie's funeral.

John and Tom were closer than most brothers-in-law,

although they didn't see each other nearly enough. He thought of him more as a blood relative, than by marriage.

Sally nodded. "Oh, we're fine. Gage wanted to see Parker, and it's been a while since we've been up, so we just took a ride."

Tom and Sally's adopted son, Gage, was just a year older than Parker. Curious, John asked, "Have you heard anything about Savannah's whereabouts? Just wondering about Murphy. I know Gage likes to see his brother when he can."

Savannah was Tom and John's friend, Cody Reynolds' wife. After Cody died, she'd struggled with the boys and life in general.

Sally shook her head. "We can't find her, or Murphy. I worry about that boy. I wish she had let us adopt him, too."

John agreed. "Yes. I know." He fiddled with an empty coffee cup on the table, thinking.

Sally ripped open the top of the bag of flour and filled a canister. "You've not been doing much cooking, have you, John?"

"Can't say that I have."

She angled her body and looked back at him. "You doing okay?"

He dropped his chin in a slow nod. "I'm hanging in there."

Sally turned back to her task. He saw her glance up at Tom, who turned back to the pan. A few silent moments passed.

John got up, went to the counter, and pulled down a clean coffee mug. He reached for the carafe. "Thanks for making this. I may need the entire pot this morning." Then he turned and faced them both. "So why don't you tell me why you are really here."

Tom lifted the last piece of bacon out of the pan and laid it on a paper towel. He moved the skillet off the burner and faced John. "We're just checking in, John. Wondering how you are doing. I know it's only been a short while since Annie left us, and it's understandable that things are still out of whack. We just wonder if there is any way we can help you out."

John sucked in a deep breath and glanced from Tom to Sally. Shaking his head slightly, he leaned back against the counter and took a sip of the hot coffee. After a moment, he said, "Some days are rougher than others. Callie's having a difficult time."

Sally patted his hand. "I spent some time with her last night. We looked through some picture albums and talked about Anne."

A lump formed in John's throat. Why hadn't he ever thought of doing that? "Thanks, Sally. I'm sure that meant a lot to her."

"It meant a lot to me. I miss her."

"I know." He nodded and tried like hell to swallow that lump. Not an easy task. "So, what time *did* you get here last night?"

"Not long after you left, apparently," Tom said. "Gage and Parker went to the barn—I think they took a quick ride up in the hills on the Gator—then later they disappeared upstairs to Parker's room to do whatever teenage boys do. Callie and Kris stuck to Sally's side."

He imagined so and looked at Sally. "Thank you. I'm sure both girls needed to be with a woman. I swear, sometimes I just don't know what to do with Callie."

"Look, John, she's a pre-teen girl and they can be just awful. Olivia, well...." She shook her head.

John asked, "Where is Olivia? She didn't come?"

"No. She's at a sleepover with a friend from her dance school. All that girl wants to do is dance. I sure hope it pays off well one day because she sure isn't doing well in school, otherwise." Sally laughed, and they both sat at the table. "But back to Callie. John, she needs a woman to talk to now and again. There's no one on this ranch except for the housecleaner and Kristin. Why don't I plan to come up a little more often, and maybe she can come and spend some long weekends with us at our ranch? What do you think? It would do Olivia good, too." She thought a moment. "And of course, Kristin is always welcome."

He figured Sally was right. "Might be a good idea. I'm not sure how to thank you."

"John Rankin, we're family. It's what we do. You can thank me by taking Gage off my hands one of these weeks. Now, that boy can be a handful."

"Anytime." He was grateful for the offer. "I can put both boys to work."

"Now that's a great idea," Tom said, then cleared his throat. "So, are you going to tell us where you were all night last night?"

John lifted his gaze to connect directly with his brother-in-law's. He pondered several responses and then replied, "No. I am not."

Chapter Seven

*A*bby watched the taillights of John's truck fade away as he rolled slowly down her street and turned left. In an instant, he was gone. Just like that.

With a sigh, she let the curtains fall back in place and stepped from the window, drawing her robe belt tighter about her waist. Absentmindedly, she drifted toward the coffee table, and picked up a paper plate with a half-eaten pizza slice. She slid it into the pizza box on top of the cold pizza. Paper plate number two followed, along with crumpled up napkins and several empty cans of Coors. She supposed she could blame it all on the beer.

No. The fault was all hers.

Time to clean up this mess.

She dumped the box and contents into the garbage can in her garage, then returned to the kitchen. Glancing about, she tried to figure out what to do next. It was barely five o'clock in the morning. She could go back to bed. Luke wouldn't be here until later this evening. She had nothing to do. Nothing but time on her hands.

Maybe wipe the crumbs up off the coffee table.

Yes. She'd do that.

She yanked at a paper towel on the holder beneath the cabinet and the entire thing tumbled down. Abby gasped, trying to capture the wayward roll of towels before it unraveled itself across the floor.

Too late.

Defeated, and with a deep exhale, she pulled out a chair and sat at her kitchen table, staring at the paper towels. Not really seeing anything.

"What in the world have I done?"

After a minute, she pushed away from the table, snatched up the towels, tore off a couple of sheets, and wiped the pizza crumbs from her coffee table. She stared at the shiny surface.

She liked John Rankin. A lot. But asking him to stay last night was a mistake.

A big one.

Wadding up the paper with crumbs inside, she headed back to the kitchen and tossed them into the garbage can under the sink.

"A mistake I am not about to repeat."

She hoped.

Who am I kidding? If he asked her out again, she'd jump at the chance like a grade school child in crush with the cutest boy in class.

Later that evening, after Tom and Sally headed back toward Billings and his kids were in bed, John sat in his bedroom staring at the television set with the sound turned off. He wasn't interested in the show and the dialogue grated on his nerves. But he didn't want to turn off the picture because for some crazy reason, the people on the set were some sort of company in the room—even if he couldn't hear them.

He'd found it difficult to get Abby off his mind for most of the day. He'd debated calling her. He had her number. Buck had given it to him after he'd arranged the blind date. That day he'd nearly thrown it away, convinced he would not go on the date to begin with.

Now, he fiddled with the piece of paper, flipping it between his fingers. Contemplating.

Finally, he picked up his landline phone and dialed.

One ring. Two. Three.

"Hello?" Abby's sweet voice floated to his ears.

He cleared his throat. "Hi Abby. It's John Rankin. I—"

"I know," she said. "How are you?"

"I'm fine."

"That's good."

"How are you?"

Silence. Awkward. "I'm fine, John. Thanks for asking."

John tried again. "Abby, I owe you an apology."

More silence. "Oh?"

He continued. "The way I left this morning was inexcusable."

"It was just uncomfortable, John. On both sides. Don't worry about it."

"I've worried about it all day, Abby."

"Well, don't. It's okay."

"I'm not so sure."

Abby didn't respond and again, the uneasy silence filled the airspace.

John plundered ahead. "I haven't been with a woman other than my wife in years, Abby. I don't know what to do in these kinds of situations. Not anymore. And really, I'm sure you don't think much of me because we'd only just met, and I was not much of a gentleman."

Her voice softened. "John, you were a perfect gentleman."

"A gentleman would have gone home. Resisted the temptation...."

"I invited you. I shouldn't have, of course. I guess it was a mistake. But I've been lonely lately, too, and I felt so comfortable with you. John, it was my fault."

"No, I shouldn't have stayed."

"I kissed you. Remember? I think that was an invitation."

"Actually, you came right out and asked me to stay."

Abby paused.

John counted the seconds.

"Yes, I did. See? You have nothing to worry about. It's all on me."

Now, that was a turn he hadn't expected. "No. I should have waited. But Abby, I have to tell you that—"

She interrupted. "It was awesome. Wasn't it? I mean, it was for me. I know we probably should have waited and all but... Well, we didn't, and it truly felt special. To me, anyway."

John closed his eyes and exhaled. He imagined her big doe eyes looking up at him. "Abby," he whispered. "It was perfect. You were wonderful. I want you to know that I don't take these things lightly and—"

She interrupted again. "John, I understand."

"You do?"

"You were my first in an awfully long time. I want you to know that. I'm not a one-night stand kind of woman. And even though I may have been a little bold, I don't take it lightly either."

Suddenly, the entire conversation seemed a little surreal. How did this happen? He'd thought she'd be mad at him for loving her and leaving so abruptly.

He could hear her breathing on the other end, then she spoke. "John, I'm going out on another limb here. Say no and my feelings won't be hurt. Would you like to have dinner at my place next Saturday night? I'll cook, and we can talk some more."

"Will your son be there?"

"No. He can stay with a friend. I'll make the arrangements. Let's leave the kids out of this for now."

John wholeheartedly agreed. "I see. Yes."

Another crossroads. Move forward or retreat?

"John?"

"Abby. I would love to."

&

THE NEXT MORNING, JOHN LOOKED UP FROM HIS HALF-EMPTY cup of coffee as Buck pushed through the back door and into his kitchen. "Get the kids off to school okay?"

"They're on the bus, at least."

"Great. Parker is the easy one. He's excited about being a junior this year."

"And the girls think they are all grown up in middle school."

John grimaced. "Hate to tell you, Buck, but they are growing up."

"Not thinking about that." He shook his head and studied the floor. After a moment, he lifted his gaze to look at John. "How are you doing, boss?"

John knew exactly what Buck was getting at. He refilled his cup of coffee and then poured a second one for Buck. "I'm good. No drama with Callie this morning, and Parker got up for school without having been told twice. Now, tomorrow will be an entirely different story." He handed Buck his coffee.

"I mean with you."

John sipped his hot brew. "I'm good. Like I said."

"What a stubborn sonofabitch you are, John Rankin. Do I have to spell it out?"

Squaring himself and facing Buck, John held his coffee cup close to his chest and glared. "I suppose you do. What's on your mind, Buck?"

"Abby! How did it go?"

John took another slow sip of his coffee. "You haven't talked to her?"

"Hell no, I haven't. What do you think I am some gossipy old woman? Besides, I don't call her. I just talk to her on Saturdays when we go into the library."

"I see."

"Well?"

"It went fine."

"Fine? What does that mean?"

John took a sip of coffee, then another. He glared at Buck. "That means things went fine. She's a genuinely pleasant woman. Smart. Good looking like you said."

"And?"

Turning away, John sat his coffee cup on the counter and headed for the door. He pulled his hat off the rack and placed it on his head. "It went fine, Buck. Now, we've got cattle to move. Let's get the boys moving and get to work."

He grinned while heading out the door as he heard Buck mumbling behind him under his breath.

Chapter Eight

*T*hat one dinner on Saturday night turned into several more over the next few weeks.

Usually, they met on the weekends when Abby's son, Luke, was with his father. It was getting increasingly harder to come up with excuses to tell his kids where he was going, but he was working it out. They'd gone to Tom and Sally's for one weekend, like Sally had suggested a while back, and Buck took all three kids camping one weekend. Other times, he simply fabricated an excuse and went with it.

He hoped to hell that didn't come back to bite him one of these days.

Sometimes they'd stay in at Abby's and she'd cook, and other times he'd take her out to eat somewhere nice in Bozeman. Occasionally, they'd catch a movie.

This weekend, they headed to the rodeo in Billings, where Buck was competing in a charity event for retired ropers and wranglers.

It wasn't Abby's favorite thing to do, John could tell, but she tolerated it. Especially since the event was for a good cause —a local horse rescue and rehabilitation center. John knew she had some aversion to rodeo because of her ex-husband, but they were there to support Buck and that seemed okay with her—if it didn't become a regular habit, or so she had said.

"His ass is too old to be out there jumping off a horse and onto those calves." John leaned into Abbey. "If he breaks his damn leg, he'll be sorry. Besides, I need him healthy on the ranch."

Abby patted his arm. "Let him be. He enjoys it. Besides, he's trying to impress that woman standing over by the fence."

John followed her gaze and spied the thirty-something looker making googly eyes at old Buck. "Hell. I'm not sure he would know what to do with her."

Laughing, Abby threw back her head. "I'm pretty sure he does."

Rotating to look at Abby, he enjoyed her smile and laughter. "How do you know so much?"

She shrugged. "I don't, really. We just chat when he brings Kris to the library."

"He ever ask you out?"

Again, she grinned. "About every other week for a year. I politely refused every time."

That surprised him. "Why?"

"Rodeo," she said, and glanced off to watch the cowboys. "I enjoy it and all, but I'm weary of the lifestyle. Luke's dad is a bronc rider. He also enjoys bucking barrel racers." She laughed. "I had eight years of rodeo and his infidelity when we were together. That was enough. So going out with Buck was not an option for me." She looked back at him. "Besides, I think I was waiting for you."

Unsure whether to be happy by that statement, or to run away fast, John knew one thing—her saying that made his heart gallop. Maybe it was time to change the subject.

"By the way," he said, breaking eye contact. "Thanks for

that book you gave me last week about helping children deal with grief. I found it helpful. Appreciate it."

Abby studied him. "Did you read any of that one for you, too?"

Clearing his throat, he glanced off, staring into the arena. "Not yet."

After a moment of silence, she reached for his hand and squeezed it. "I'm glad the book for Callie was helpful, John."

LATER THAT EVENING, OVER BURGERS AT A PUB CLOSE TO THE arena in Billings, Abby raised another subject that surprised him, saying she thought it was time to "Take things to the next level." Pausing, he slowly placed his beer on the paper coaster on the table and lifted his gaze to make eye contact.

"What are you saying, Abby?"

Leaning across the table, she elaborated. "John, it's been a couple of months since we've been seeing each other. Don't you think it's time we tell the kids?" She peered at him over her beer, while picking at her French fries.

He'd thought he could keep Abby his little secret— evidently not. "It's too soon, Abby."

She sighed. "So how long do you think you can keep sneaking me off to Bozeman or Billings, where no one knows us? I feel like you're hiding me. Is it the kids, or is it really me?"

He felt stunned at her words. "Hell, Abby. It's not you."

"It's not? Well, maybe then, it's you."

Shaking his head, he said, "No, it's the kids. All three of them. We need to wait."

Sitting back, she glared. "John Rankin, it's you. What are you afraid of?"

Those words took him aback. "I—"

Abby gently slapped the table in front of him, interrupting.

"Now don't you go saying you're not afraid, John Rankin. Tell me."

Damn, she knew him already. Just like Annie did.

He cleared his throat. "Abby, making us public… Well, it means dealing with the kids. And it means we have to tell people when they see us out. You know how these kinds of things can get."

Her facial expressions didn't move. "No, I guess I don't. Tell me."

"Sure, you do. People talk."

"And?"

"Well, they will say things."

"Like?"

He blinked. Was she challenging him? Suddenly, he wasn't sure how to respond. Shifting in his seat, he stared at the wooden tabletop for a few seconds, then lifted his gaze. "Abby, you know, the gossip."

She leaned in. "Are we doing anything wrong, John?"

"Of course not."

"Then you feel guilty."

"Me? Why?"

"Because of Anne. People will say it's too soon and tsk-tsk behind your back. People will wonder who I am. How you met me. They will ask questions and you are not sure how you will respond. People will say what a shame it was that you couldn't wait to replace Anne. I can go on. Should I?"

He sat back. "No. Yes. All that."

"We are doing nothing wrong, John."

"I know."

"But you're not ready to say *to hell with what people will think.* You're not ready to walk into a restaurant in Livingston with me on your arm and introduce me to your friends. And of course, you're not ready to introduce me to your kids."

"Well, I've not met Luke yet, either."

"But he knows about you. Do Callie and Parker even know about me?"

Stunned, John sat back and perused her. She'd told Luke about him? He'd not dared broach the subject with Callie and Parker. "I, uh… No, Abby. They don't know about you."

"Is there a reason?"

"Not really. I just—"

"I see." Her head ticked. "Do you have any plans to tell them? Or is that not even on your radar?"

To be honest, he hadn't considered it. Should he have? It had only been a couple of months. But he couldn't tell her that, could he?

He had to. "Abby, I'm not ready."

She straightened in her seat, sucked in a breath, and held it. For a moment, she glanced into the restaurant crowd, as if carefully measuring her next words. Hell, she likely was. Finally, with an exhale, she faced him. "I understand."

Standing, she dropped her napkin on the table, holding his gaze. "And that's okay. When you are ready, John, let me know. I think you need to take me home now."

She turned and headed toward the exit.

John stood and tossed a hundred-dollar bill on the table, then followed her out. He tried to hold her hand on the walk back to the truck, but she gently pulled it away and pushed it into her jacket pocket.

That didn't sit well with him, tugging at his heartstrings.

The drive home from Billings to her home in Livingston was a long and silent ride. When he pulled into her driveway, he turned toward her. "Abby, talk to me for a minute."

She stared out the passenger side window. "I don't really have anything more to say, John."

"If I hurt you, I'm sorry."

She sniffled. "I somehow feel rejected and I'm not sure

what to do with those feelings. Don't mind me," she said, and continued staring out the window.

"Dammit." The word slurred on a breath. "I didn't mean to make you feel bad. Please believe me when I say it has nothing to do with you, Abby."

She whirled, looking at him. "It has everything to do with me, John!" Finally, she looked directly at him. That's when he saw the tears. *Hell.*

"Oh, Abby…." With a forefinger, he smoothed a few tears on her cheek. "I'm sorry. I'm just not good at this relationship thing. You're better off without me."

A frantic expression raced across her face, and she grasped his hand. "Oh, John. That's not true. My life has never been better these past few weeks. I can be patient. You know best about your kids. I just need to know that we are going to get there one of these days soon."

She searched his eyes, and John didn't know what for, but he figured she needed some sort of reassurance from him. The one thing he knew, though, was that he had enjoyed every minute of the past two months spent with her.

"Yes. I know them. And I also know me, and that I procrastinate sometimes on things that are important because I don't want to deal with them. My kids are fine. You're right. I need to tell them about you, and then we can go from there."

She smiled and nodded. "One step at a time."

John thought a moment. "Abby, there's a BBQ and hayride out at the Carson ranch two weeks from tomorrow. My family and my friends will all be there. Would you like to come? Bring Luke too."

"I would love that. But only if you are ready."

He nodded. "I'll be ready by then. Promise."

"Okay."

She leaned toward him, and he gathered her into his arms.

Chapter Nine

*B*uck agreed it would be better for Parker and Callie to meet Abby in a group setting. The community hayride was perfect. The Carson's held it every fall over at their ranch, and everyone pitched in with food, drinks, and entertainment. There would be pumpkin carving for the children, music for all ages, and the hayride, of course. They'd not missed it in years, and John had finally reconciled the fact that it was as good a place as any for him to introduce the kids to Abby.

Except for the unexpected resistance on the home front, and that he'd put off telling Callie. He had talked with Parker a week earlier—he appeared to take it fine, the boy telling him he'd already suspected something—but who knew with teenage boys.

Now, he had to break the news to his daughter—if he could get past the current argument.

"I don't care about any stupid hayride. I'm not going."

John stood in his daughter's doorway, knowing he was about to embark on another struggle. Perhaps he should have laid down the law months earlier, because he couldn't let this go any longer. His voice raised. "Calandra Rankin! Get up, get dressed, and get downstairs in five minutes. We go to the Carson's BBQ every year and this year is no different."

"Not me."

John's head ticked to the side. "All right. Then you'll go as you are." He stepped into the room, scooped his pajama-clad daughter into his arms, and headed for the hallway. "I'm sure some of your classmates will love to see your new pajamas."

Callie shrieked. "Daddy! Put me down. No."

He halted at the top of the stair and looked at his daughter. "Callie, I don't have time for your shenanigans. Do you hear me? Tonight, we are doing this my way." He set her down on the landing. "Now, get back in your room and get dressed. I want you downstairs pronto. No more of this."

Callie huffed and rolled her eyes, then trotted off, muttering. "I don't really wanna meet your new girlfriend, *Dad.*"

Whoa. "Callie?"

She halted.

"What did you say?"

Rotating back, she stared at him. "I only have five minutes to get dressed, *Dad.*"

Dad? What happened to Daddy? "What did you say?"

Her shoulders rose and fell. "I said I don't wanna meet your new girlfriend." Then she turned and raced into her room, slamming the door behind her.

Shit.

This was a bad idea all the way around.

Hell, he didn't even know Callie knew anything about Abby.

Girlfriend?

He stepped forward with a firm rap on Callie's door.

"I'm getting dressed," she yelled out.

John lowered his hand. "I'll be right here. Callie, we need to talk."

He waited at least five minutes, then she opened the door. John sighed and asked if he could come in. Callie stepped back, and he entered his daughter's room. "Let's sit." He grasped Callie's hand and pulled her along with him. They sat side-by-side on the bed.

John glanced at his daughter. She'd dressed in jeans, her favorite boots, and a western snap-front shirt. Standard wardrobe. "Thanks for getting dressed," he told her. "You've been up here in your room all day. I want you to eat something before we go. I'm worried about you not eating."

Callie exhaled and reached to the top drawer of her bedside table and pulled it open. John spied the contents, then looked at his daughter. She shrugged and grinned back. The drawer was full of half-eaten bags and boxes of snack foods.

"Well, that explains the missing items from the pantry. But you need to eat more than snacks."

She shrugged her shoulders again.

"Callie…."

"I ate something."

"All right." He would fight that battle another day. "But look, we need to talk. Seriously talk, Callie. Look at me."

She didn't respond. John lifted her chin with his forefinger to bring her gaze to his. One corner of her mouth curled up. "Okay."

"You know I loved your mama more than my own life," he said. "And you know I love you just as much. None of that is ever going to change."

She nodded. "I know Daddy."

"But we must move forward, honey. Your mama isn't here anymore—not her body anyway—but her soul and her memories are all around us. And everything she was for us, and with us, while she was on earth—well, we just need to keep all of that in our hearts every single day. We still live our lives, Callie. Your mama would want you to be happy."

She sniffed and rubbed a finger underneath her nose. "I know."

"Callie, no one ever will replace your mama in my heart. Or in yours."

She nodded. "But you have a girlfriend."

"And how did you hear about that?"

"Kris."

He arched a brow. "How is that?"

"She heard you and her dad talking in the barn and she told me."

So that was it. "All right." He shifted so he could really look into her eyes. "Callie, I'm spending some time with someone. That only means we are going out to dinner occasionally, a movie, dinner. We enjoy each other's company. I don't know if there will be anything else."

"Are you going to marry her?"

"I have no plans to marry anyone right now, Callie. All I want to do tonight is let you meet her. Maybe you'll feel better if you do."

She shrugged. "Probably not."

"I understand, and that's okay."

"I'll say hello."

"That's my girl."

"It will all be okay, Callie."

She shrugged again. "If you say so, *Dad*."

John took and deep breath and slowly exhaled. This was going to be a long night.

JOHN WATCHED THE DIRT ROAD LEADING BACK TO THE CARSON'S Ranch for Abby's Chevy Blazer. He'd got Callie and Parker out of the house without further incident—a little later than planned, but at least they were there. Earlier that afternoon, he'd made potato salad and baked brownies—and had managed to get their contributions to the food tables.

One task done.

Times like these he appreciated Annie, and all she had done over the years getting ready for family outings and get-togethers at the ranch. He sometimes wondered if he'd ever acknowledged all she did, day after day. Had he ever told her how much he appreciated her?

Surely he had. But now, he couldn't recall a single time. He sure hoped she never thought he was taking advantage of her. She never complained. Not one time. She always took everything in stride.

Well, he did his best by her, and he hoped that was enough. Maybe he learned some lessons he could apply to the future.

That remained to be seen.

His brownies might not be the best, and he was sure the potato salad had too much mustard, but he'd made the effort and was pleased enough with the end products. Callie had even perked up on the ride over, carried the brownies to the dessert table, and then disappeared with Kris and her other friends.

Good. She'd be fine, he was certain.

Abby was late. He hoped everything was okay.

He scanned the crowd again and settled on his son, smiling as he watched him roughhousing with his friends near the barn. Immediately, he wondered where the years had gone. Seemed only yesterday that he was the sixteen-year-old, roughhousing with Tom and Cody. The threesome had been a rowdy group and got into more trouble than he liked to remember.

Cody was the wild card. His death hit both him and Tom hard. The drunk driver had been Cody, himself, and he took out half a family with him, driving too many miles over the speed limit on a back road, with too many whiskey sours inside him.

Cody's death devastated his young wife, Savannah, leaving her behind with their two young boys, Gage and Murphy. The whole thing was tragic. But no more tragic than Savannah resorting to alcohol to get through the day-to-day, and other addictions to support her children over the next few years. That's when Tom and John stepped in and convinced Savannah to let Tom and Sally adopt Gage. But she just couldn't give up Murphy, telling them it would be easier for her to handle one child. She'd disappear from time to time, and when she did, all everyone could do was pray the boy was safe —then more recently, they'd found out Murphy had been removed from Savannah's home and placed in foster care.

Where? John had no clue. He wished he knew. He'd take the boy in himself if he could find him.

Movement to his right pulled him out of his contemplation. He smiled as Abby stepped out of her vehicle, then reached back inside for a dish. Her son, Luke, rounded the truck with a bag of chips in his hands.

Abby approached him, smiling, and his heart swelled. He moved toward her and took the dish out of her hands as he leaned in to place a quick kiss on her cheek. He pulled back, and she looked up into his eyes, his chest full of his ever-expanding heart.

"You are a sight for sore eyes," he told her.

Abby smiled wider and her eyes twinkled. "It's good to see you, John."

"I'm so glad you are here." And he was. He felt alive again, for the first time in months. "Let's get this food over to the table."

But before he stepped away, he remembered Luke. Juggling the dish, he put out his hand. "This handsome young man must be Luke."

The boy beamed and shook John's hand. "Yes sir. Nice to meet you."

"And you, too." John glanced about. "I'm sure glad you came here with your mama. There's a passel of kids around here, somewhere."

Luke's eyes were already moving over the crowd. He turned to his mother. "Mama, I think I see some kids from school over there. Can I go?"

Abby took the chips out of his hand. "Go. Shoo!"

Then Luke was off, and John turned to Abby and looked deep into her eyes again. "I've missed you something awful this week."

Her upturned face and cheerful smile were nearly his undoing. "I don't think I could have made it through another day, John."

When the hayride wrapped up, and everyone's bellies were full, the evening quieted into dusk with a bonfire and singing. Cowboys and guitars and lonesome, soulful songs of the west filled the night. Abby leaned into John as they sat on a log near the fire, and he put his arms around her. They sat somewhat isolated from the rest of the crowd, and he liked the fact that they were getting a little alone time after this hectic day.

"Cold?"

"No. This is perfect," she said.

John let the moment sink in. It had been a wonderful late afternoon and evening. He had enjoyed Abby's company so much, and she had fallen right in with his friends and their wives. Of course, they'd only had glimpses of Callie the past few hours, and he had a feeling she was avoiding him. Parker met Abby earlier and was amiable and polite, if not a little uncomfortable. He supposed that was to be expected.

The boy was quiet and kept to himself at home most of the time. Maybe more so since Annie died. Or he was out on the ranch on his horse. He sure hoped his quietness wasn't as much of a red flag as Callie's rebellion.

"Seen the kids lately?" Abby asked.

John cleared his throat. "Parker is over there with the teenagers. Last I saw of Luke, he was tagging along behind with them. Callie? I'm not so sure."

"Yes, Luke is idolizing those older boys. Of course, they are all into rodeo and you know he's all about that. His father, and all."

"Of course."

"I saw Callie a few minutes ago," Abby added. "She was at the dessert table with a couple of girls. I said a quick hello, but she turned and fled. And then…" she paused and pointed. "Oh, there she is, sitting on that hay wagon over there."

John squinted beyond the fire. Yes, there was his girl, sitting in the middle of a string of girls her age on the wagon, swinging their legs and watching the boys.

"I want you to meet her before we leave," he said.

"I'm looking forward to it, but if it doesn't happen today, John, let's not push it." She turned slightly, so she could look into his face. "At least she knows about me now and sees us together. I think it's important that we just meet soon. Nothing more. No expectations. I don't want her to think I'm trying to take her mother's place."

John put his finger on Abby's lips. "Sh… I understand. I know you would never, but Callie can be unpredictable. I want you to know that."

She nodded. "That's for another time." She sat up straighter then and turned to face him. "But there is a conversation you and I need to have soon. And, with all our children at some point, not long after that."

She bit her lip. Her mood flipped a switch.

A queasy sensation hit John's gut and, abruptly, he knew something was wrong. "Abby, what is it?"

She sighed and her shoulders dropped. "I feel like such a damn fool. I should have known better."

That alarmed him. "Known better how?"

She searched his face for a long moment. "John, we need to talk. Probably now is not the best of times, but soon. There is something serious we need to discuss."

Hell. She was breaking up with him. He shouldn't have gotten so attached. Had she and Luke's father gotten back together? Surely not. Maybe she met someone else. Maybe she realized he's just a middle-aged, lonely man who has nothing to offer.

"Abby, are you trying to tell me you don't want to see me?"

She held his gaze, then pushed out a breath. "No, John. I'm not. I can't imagine not seeing you."

"Then what?"

Her lips clamped shut tight. She perused his face.

"Abby…."

Taking a deep breath, Abby closed her eyes and exhaled. Blinking them open again, she said quietly, "John, I'm pregnant. I think it must have happened that first night. We weren't so careful."

Stunned, he stared at her, thinking back. "Pregnant?"

"Yes."

"You're sure."

"I'm positive."

"A baby."

"Yes, that's the result of pregnancy."

John cleared his throat and stood, taking a few steps away and staring off for a moment into the fire. "Hell, I'm too old for this. What the…."

Then he whirled back and looked at Abby's scared face. "Hell, Abby. I'm sorry. Are you okay? How long have you known? I didn't mean to be so damn insensitive."

She stood and took a step toward him. "I'm fine. I've a little more time to process this than you."

"So, you've known a while?"

"Two days."

"Why didn't you call me?"

It was her turn to glance off this time. After a moment, she faced him. "I needed the time to think, John. I knew I would see you this weekend."

He reached for her hands. Without further thought, blurted out, "We'll get married. Soon. I'll get on that tomorrow."

Abby pulled her hands away. "Get on that? Great." She narrowed her gaze. "Because it's the right thing to do?"

"Well, of course, Abby."

Closing her eyes, she blew out a long breath. "I think not, John Rankin."

Chapter Ten

 ne month later....

JOHN STOOD ON THE BED OF THE PICKUP TRUCK, BROKE OPEN A square bale of hay, and threw half of it out the back to the ground. The cattle made a line following the truck, some waiting for their feed, others slowly chewing as they pulled the grass into their mouths. Buck drove the truck slowly as John continued to bust bales and push the hay out for the animals. Down the hill, Parker and one of the ranch hands were doing the same thing, feeding another row of cows.

A crisp whip of wind blew his collar up and teased at this hat. Soon they'd be doing this in colder weather and snow, if they didn't get this herd moved closer to the fields with the larger round bales of hay.

He didn't look forward to winter. The older he got, the more he disliked ranching in the winter, but he'd get out and do it if his bones would let him. An idle cowboy was not a healthy cowboy.

Winters were hard on the ranch, but the cattle needed fed and cared for. Every day. The mamas needed nourishment for the babies that would come in the spring.

Babies in the spring.

Buck slowed the truck and John stood up, looking out over the ranch, not really seeing anything. By his rough calculations, he and Abby would have a baby of their own, maybe late May or early June.

He wished he knew exactly what was going on with her. She refused to talk to him.

Oh, he had tried. He'd called, and she'd politely said she couldn't talk right then, that she needed time. He'd stopped by twice, but she didn't answer the door, although he knew she was home, her Blazer parked outside. Lately, she'd not picked up the phone either.

He'd waited for her once outside the library. Watched her leave, but never approached her. That felt a little too much like stalking. That was not his intent.

But he had to talk to her.

Women! He was not good at understanding them. Once he'd understood how Annie ticked, he hadn't had to worry about other women. How had he screwed up with Abby? He thought he'd done the right thing, saying they would get married. It was the honorable thing, and well, dammit, even more, it was what he wanted.

He'd fallen head over heels in love with her. A new baby would just be icing on the cake. He wanted to take care of her and their child. All their children.

Yet, he could understand her reasoning. Her hesitation. She wasn't just taking on him. She was taking on a whole new family and a ranch. And the first time she'd married, it hadn't turned out so well.

A blended family. Could they do it?

Was he too old to start over? How did she even feel about that?

Buck came to a full stop. John jumped down from the tailgate. He brushed hay from his clothes and then moved toward the cab. Buck got out and faced him. "Penny for your thoughts, boss. You were looking mighty contemplative there, a few seconds ago."

John stood, hands on hips, and stared at the ground. "I'll never understand women, Buck."

He glanced up to see Buck rear back and cackle. "You think any of us understand them?"

John blew out a breath and watched it fan out on the chilly breeze. "Yeah. You're right. Let's head back to the house."

He turned to round the truck for the other side, but Buck put out a hand to stop him. "John. Hold up a minute."

John rotated back to look his friend square in the eyes. Buck continued, "You've been mighty quiet the past weeks. Need to talk?"

John narrowed his gaze. "Have you talked to her?"

He shook his head. "No. Well, barely. We haven't been to the library lately—I bought Kris a stack of books for her birthday, so she's reading those—but I caught up with Abby at the grocery store a few days ago. She blew me off when I asked if the two of you were going to the country club for the half-way house fund-raising shindig next weekend. She wouldn't look me in the eye and turned, shaking her head. I take it she didn't want to talk about it, and she especially didn't want to talk about you."

John sucked in air and held it, his chest expanding. He paused and then lifted his chin. Finally, he let out a slow breath. "I have told no one about this, Buck, and it goes no further than right here—but Abby and I, well, we've got a serious problem."

Buck narrowed his gaze. "You need my help?"

Glancing off, John returned, "Hell, no. I have to figure this thing out myself."

"What is it, John?"

He looked back into Buck's face. "Abby is pregnant."

After a moment, Buck exhaled, whistling through his teeth. "I take it the baby is yours."

John exploded. "Hell, yes, it's mine." He punched the fender of the truck and headed for the passenger side door and got in, slamming it. "Let's go, Buck!"

Buck joined him in the cab, started the truck, and headed down the hill toward the house. Finally, he said, "You ask her to marry you?"

"Yeah, I did. Of course. I told her we would."

"And what did she say?"

Buck kept staring straight ahead. John turned to look out his window. "She said no. She won't marry me."

Buck chewed on that a moment. "She's got her pride."

"Pride?" John twisted in the seat. "What the hell does pride have to do with it? She's pregnant no matter what, with or without a husband. Where does pride come in when she's raising a baby on her own? *My baby?* I don't know what she is thinking."

He looked back out the window to his right. Buck kept driving. Soon, they reached the barn and pulled up out back. They both exited and headed inside.

"John, one second."

John knew his friend had his best interest in mind, but he wasn't sure he could talk about this any longer. He had turned it over internally for weeks, calling himself every kind of fool for getting himself—and Abby—into this predicament. And with Annie not even in the grave a year yet. How would his kids handle this? That worried him most. The conversation he'd had with Callie recently haunted him.

"Look, Buck. I've twisted this thing every which way but

loose for days, repeatedly. I just don't know what to do. I've told her I'd marry her. I've tried to call her and even stopped by to see her in person, but she refuses to talk. And if she married me, it's probably a solution to one problem and maybe the start of others, considering the Callie situation and all. I just don't know."

Buck studied him. "I'm sure you are right. This is not a simple decision, one way or the other. There are consequences either way, I suppose."

"She's not raising my child without me. I won't have it." He stared off into the distance.

"That's very nineteen-sixties of you, John."

He whipped his head around. "What the hell does that mean?"

Buck stepped closer. "It means your attitude is a little old-fashioned. Women raise kids on their own these days all the time and pretty much every woman I know of would say that having a kid doesn't mean you automatically get married. Abby has a respectable job, and she's an independent woman."

"True, but—"

Buck stepped closer. "John, you want her because she wants to be with you, because she loves you. And she wants the same. No woman wants to feel like an obligation."

"I would never do that."

"Ah, but you did."

"What?"

"You made her feel like an obligation."

"She told you that?"

Buck shook his head. "No. She didn't have to. You said it."

John stepped back and shoved his hands into his pockets. "Shit."

"Yep. And you stepped in it. Welcome to the twenty-first century, boss."

John shook his head. "But she knows getting married is what we need to do."

"*Need to do.* You told her that?"

"I did. I told her the night she told me she was pregnant. And, I left her a damn phone message saying the same because she wouldn't pick up. So, she might as well just give in and marry me."

Buck stepped back, eyeing him. "So, when you told her all that, you didn't go all rough stock cowboy on her, did you? Some women just don't respond well to that kind of bullshit."

"I simply told her we'd marry, Buck. What else was I to do?"

"Propose?"

"What?"

"You *told* her you'd marry her. You've said more than once, now. *Told her.* Did you ever think about simply proposing? *Asking* for her hand in marriage, romantically speaking? Giving her a choice and a chance to respond? Women like that kind of shit, you know. Ever think of that?"

John stared at Buck, dumbfounded. No, he hadn't thought of that at all.

ABBY PULLED A COUPLE OF BOOKS OUT OF HER TOTE BAG AND slipped them onto the shelving cart. Her fingers lingered over the book on the top, *Naming Your Baby*, and the one underneath it, *A Guide for Single Mothers*. Quickly, she shuffled the books around on the cart so those two wouldn't be on top. The queasiness in her tummy returned then, and she rubbed her abdomen with her right hand.

Morning sickness had not been her friend the past couple of weeks. Turning, she headed for the women's restroom, picking up her pace as she neared the entrance. Barely making it inside, she locked the door behind her and lost her breakfast in the next instant. After a moment, she flushed and lowered the lid on the commode and sat there for a while, wiping her mouth with a damp paper towel and a shaky hand.

A knock came at the door. "Abby? Are you okay?"

"I'm fine, Grace."

"Are you sure? You looked a little green when you rushed by me."

Goodness. I didn't even see her. "I'm fine. I'll be out in a minute."

"Okay, sweetie. I'm a little worried about you."

Abby waited for a moment, then rose and unlocked the door. Peeking out, she saw that Grace, head librarian and her friend, still stood outside the door. Abby reached for her hand and pulled her inside the small one-person restroom and locked the door again behind them.

"Abby, what in the world is going on?" The look on Grace's face was one of concern.

Abby blew out a hard breath. She couldn't keep the secret any longer. "I'm pregnant."

"What the...? Abby!"

"I'm thirty-five and I'm single and I'm pregnant. I guess you need to know since you are my boss, and I may need to take leave down the road."

Grace took her hand. "Oh, my goodness, Abby. What happened?"

Abby arched a brow.

"Well, I know what happened, but...."

Abby plunged ahead. She needed to talk to someone about this. Grace was her only choice. "I've been seeing someone. We hadn't really told anyone because of his kids and all. And because it hasn't been that long since his wife died. And frankly, he's having issues with all of that, and do you know what? He said, *We'll get married*, like it was a duty or something. I told him no and I haven't talked to him since."

"Oh, Abby."

"I know."

"Has he called?"

"Oh, every day. He leaves messages."

"And you don't pick up or call back?"

"No."

"Why not?"

Abby sucked in a breath. "Because I don't want to be anyone's obligation, Grace. I don't want to force this. It was hard enough for him to consider telling his kids about us—which just recently happened—but now we have to tell them about a baby?"

Grace frowned. "Abby, are you thinking clearly? This baby is coming if you tell the kids, or not. They will find out eventually."

"Maybe I'll move."

Narrowing her gaze, Grace shook her head. "And take the baby away from the father? That's not fair to anyone. Frankly, that doesn't sound like you, Abby."

Deflating to sit on the commode lid again, Abby exhaled. "No, that's not me. Stupid idea. But I will not marry him just because he says so, like it's a check in the box."

"Oh goodness, Abby. Really? Who is this mystery man, anyway?"

"I can't tell you."

"It's Buck McGinnis, isn't it?"

"Oh, good Lord no."

"Then it must be John Rankin."

Abby jumped up. "Why would you say that?"

Grace crossed her arms over her chest and smiled. "Because I overheard you talking with Buck a few weeks ago. And while I don't know him, I know of him—who doesn't?—

and I remember he lost his wife back in the spring. Now, Abby Cooper, I want you to promise something."

"Look, Grace. I can't really promise anything to anyone. My life is a train wreck and I'm exhausted and honestly scared to death about the future. I may throw up again at any moment and...."

"Abby, stop talking. Look at me."

Abby clamped her mouth shut.

"Just promise me this one thing. If John Rankin calls you back again, pick up the damn phone and talk to him."

"That's all?"

"Yes. He deserves it and so do you."

Abby chewed her lip. "It's been a month. I suppose I should talk to him."

"You could call him."

Abby furiously shook her head. "No. He will call and I'll pick up."

"Good." Grace patted her hands. "And in the meantime, consider that he's likely scared, too. Probably damn scared. So cut him a little slack. Okay?"

"Okay." Abby pondered that thought. John scared? Oh hell. She'd only been thinking of herself. How must John be feeling about everything right now?

JOHN KNEW WHAT HE HAD TO DO, BUT BEFORE HE COULD SET things into motion, there was something else that needed his attention. He wasn't sure which would be easier—proposing to Abby or telling Callie and Parker what he was about to do.

He supposed he needed to ask them, too. Not tell them.

The thought of an actual proposal to Abby had warmed his heart and made him excited at the prospect of their future together. He could only hope that Abby's heart would take a turn and agree.

But first—

"Callie? Parker!" Standing at the foot of the stairs, John called up. "Need to talk to you two for a moment."

Parker bounded down the stairs first, followed by a slow-moving Callie. John watched her take one step at a time and then roll her eyes as she came eye-level with him. "What did I do now, Daddy?"

He smiled. "Nothing, pumpkin. I just need to talk to you both. Ask you something, actually."

"Hm." Callie skipped down the last few steps and headed through the kitchen.

"Head on into the great room." He followed her in and sat on the ottoman in front of the sofa. Both his children sat facing him.

"What's up, Dad?"

John cleared his throat. "I have something important to ask the two of you."

"Oh?" Callie tipped her head to the side.

"Yes."

He exhaled, an act he hoped would settle his nerves. Leaning forward, he made a tent with his hands and fingers, his elbows on his knees. Nervously, he tapped his fingers together.

"Kids, please hear me out before you interrupt me. Okay?"

They both fixed their gazes on him and nodded. He sure as hell hoped they would let him say his piece before getting upset. Especially Callie.

"You both know I loved your mama more than my own life. I know she's only been gone about half a year now, but—"

"But you and Abby are getting married, aren't you, Dad?"

John turned his direction toward his normally quiet son. Parker, who for all these months had not given him one iota of trouble, and who hadn't weighed in at all about him dating Abby, had spoken up.

He nodded, then looked from Parker to Callie. "I'm asking for your permission to ask Abby to marry me. To become part of our family. I've not proposed to her, and I would like to, but I need your blessing. I won't do it if either of you says you don't want me to."

Silence followed. He watched his daughter stare ahead, and then turn to her left to look at her older brother. Parker gave her a quick glance, then back to his father and said, "Do you love her, Dad?"

John dipped his head. "I do. It wasn't something I expected to happen at all, or this fast. I really didn't go looking to fall in love. Abby is a friend of Buck's and it just happened. You know that—"

Callie interrupted. "Do you love her like you loved Mommy?"

John looked straight into Callie's eyes. "No, honey. I will love no one like I loved your Mama. She will always be special in my heart and in yours and Parker's. That love is only reserved for the four of us, and no one will ever take that away."

"But you still love Abby."

"I do. I love her in a different way."

"In an Abby way."

"I guess you could say that."

Callie thought about that. John waited. But it was Parker who spoke up again next. "I have questions, Dad."

John leaned forward. "Then ask them. Now is the time for us to talk about this."

Parker nodded. "All right. Will Abby move here? What about her son, Luke? I suppose if she comes, he will too. Does that make us all family? Do I have to share a room with him?"

John exhaled. "That's a lot of questions but let me see how

I do." He watched Parker, but also noticed Callie's interest and that she was hanging on every word.

"I've discussed none of this with Abby yet, of course, but I am assuming she would move to the ranch. So yes, she would live here with us. Luke, too. As to sharing a room, no. We'll figure something out. You're pushing seventeen and deserve space of your own, Parker. You'll not have to share."

"That Luke ain't staying with me." Callie piped up.

John laughed. "No, Callie. Luke won't be sharing your room either. Don't you worry about that."

"There's that space over the barn," Parker said. "Next to Buck and Kris's apartment. We talked about that for me a while back."

John nodded. "That we did. You're probably old enough. Let's discuss that later, though."

"All right, Dad."

Callie sighed. "That Luke needs to stay out of my stuff."

"No one is getting into your stuff, Callie. I promise."

Another wave of silence hung over the three of them. Finally, John said, "So, what do you think? I know there will be some getting used to. We'll have to figure some things out and it will all be new to Abby and Luke, too. There will be adjustments. But we can work through it, right? And heck, it might be fun, even."

"I'm still deciding in my head if it's okay," Callie said.

Parker stared at her, then looked to John. "Will it make you happy, Dad, to marry her?"

Something clutched in his chest as he took in Parker's question. Suddenly, the boy seemed more like a young man. Hell, he was. "Yes, son. It would make me happy. I've been lonely since your Mama… And I've enjoyed Abby's company. In fact, your Mana was insistent that I do not live out the rest of my life alone. She knew me only too well."

"How so?" Parker asked with interest.

"You'll find out one day that a man needs a woman beside him, son. No one will ever replace your Mama, of course, but it would be nice to be happy again."

Parker studied him. "Then it's okay with me."

Bless you, son. He nodded. "Thank you, Parker."

"I'm still thinking." Callie said. She glanced to her left when Parker gave her shoulder a nudge. "What?"

"It's okay, Callie. We can handle this. It will make Dad happy."

Callie turned to her father, a slow grin spreading over her face. "I want you to be happy again, Daddy. Because when you are happy, I am happy. I'm still thinking, but I think it will be okay. I'll never forget Mommy and I'm just saying that Abby will never be like my Mommy. Okay?"

"Of course." John closed his eyes and felt his shoulders fall. In the next instant, both Callie and Parker were on either side of him, and he reached around to pull them close. He might have even shed a tear while they weren't looking.

"Callie-girl, your Mama will always be your Mama, and no one could ever take her place. Abby will be kind of like a bonus mom. Will that work?"

Pulling back, Callie searched his eyes. John felt her sincerity straight through to his soul. "A bonus mom? Yes. That's kind of cool." She smiled, and the warmth shot straight down to his toes.

Chapter Eleven

*J*ohn stood in front of the library. He did not know if what he'd planned would work. This could all go wrong. Very wrong. Or it could go very right. Either way, he had to get on with it.

Pushing through the double glass doors, he stepped into an enclosed entrance and then into the building. A few kids and adults mingled about—more people than he had expected at this time of day. He supposed he should check in at the desk to see where Abby might be, and if it was possible to see her.

But as he stepped further into the space, he saw Abby standing behind the counter talking with a co-worker while she opened some boxes of books. Suddenly, the front door flew open and kids were everywhere. School was out, he guessed. Hell, this was a bad time. He shifted the bouquet of roses in his hands and nervously sidestepped an older couple leaving.

Damn, he was just standing there in the way.

Focused on Abby though, he stood frozen to the spot, watching as she continued to pull books out of a shipping box, glance over the spines, and place on the cart. She lifted her gaze and chatted quietly with the co-worker. He could hear her voice but didn't comprehend a single word she said.

She looked so pretty standing there. Her auburn hair shimmered with golden highlights, reflecting the sunlight streaming in from the large library windows. He stepped closer to the counter and watched her full lips move as she spoke, and her blue eyes dart back and forth from the books to the other person.

There is the mother of my child.

He loved her. His heart swelled in his chest as he watched her. So mesmerized, he didn't notice anyone else coming through the door, and he was quickly shuffled aside as kids and adults weaved in and out around him.

He had to wonder how pitiful he looked, standing there staring at her, heartsick, with a bunch of roses in his hand. A big, dumb cowboy looking mighty out of place, pining away for the woman he loved. A woman who was not giving him one bit of attention and had no clue he was even in the room.

"Sorry. I didn't mean to bump you, sir. May I help you?"

He looked at a young man standing beside him, who was now stepping back. "No," John said. "I mean, yes, thank you. I'm here to…. Um. I want to see…."

What the hell am I doing here? This is a mistake. I should have done this another way.

He turned to leave, stepping away from the desk area.

"John?"

Abby.

He swiveled back and leveled his gaze. She had moved from behind the desk now and closer to him. All he could do was look at her, a lump in his throat the size of Yellowstone.

"John?" she repeated, a curious look on her face.

He breathed. Finally. "Abby. You're busy. I should come back. When would be a better time?"

She ignored his question. "You haven't called the past couple of days."

He shook his head. "No. No, I haven't. I was beginning to feel like a stalker and besides, I knew you wouldn't pick up."

"I was going to pick up. I was waiting for you to call."

He straightened his shoulders and squared himself in front of her. "You were?"

"Yes."

"Damn." He glanced about, lowering his voice. "I mean, darn it. I can't seem to get things right."

She didn't respond, just stood there looking at him. Suddenly, he felt incredibly awkward. He should leave. "I should—"

"Are those roses for me?" Her eyes were full of question and probable expectation.

His heart was full of hope.

He glanced about. Suddenly everyone's eyes—a bunch of kids and some adults, probably Abby's co-workers—were on the two of them. He looked at Abby. Reaching for her hand, he drew closer to her.

"Yes, Abby," he breathed. "These roses are for you. I remembered you liked the last bunch I gave you." He handed them to her.

She gathered them into her hands and brought them to her nose. "They smell wonderful. Thank you."

Her lashes fluttered as she looked up at him. His heart leaped. Damn. "I can't prolong this any longer," he muttered. Then he got down on one knee.

A collective gasp rippled throughout the room.

Abby blinked, watching him, and cradled the roses in her right arm.

John took her left hand.

"Abby Cooper," he began, "I know we've only known each other a short time, but I love you with all of my heart. I don't want to spend another day away from you. I want to spend all our days and nights together for the rest of our lives." He cleared his throat and stared into Abby's eyes—eyes that were tearing up.

"Abby, I love you. Will you marry me?"

Oh please, God, do not let her say no.

He watched a tear amble down her cheek and settle near the corner of her mouth. "You love me? Truly?" she asked.

"With all of my heart."

"But your kids?"

He nodded. "They are fine. Callie said you could be her bonus mom."

That made Abby choke up a little. "Oh, John… I need to talk to Luke."

"I understand. Of course. But what do *you* want?"

She pulled her lower lip into her mouth.

"Abby. Please. I'm asking, not telling. Hell, I might be begging. Marry me?"

She smiled and gripped his hand, and then John remembered the ring. He reached into his pocket, pulled out the small black velvet box, and flipped open the lid. He'd been to Billings and back yesterday and bought the biggest damn diamond he could find.

Abby gasped. "Oh, my."

"Yeah, it's big and flashy," he said, "but it still can't measure up to how big my love is for you, darling."

Abby blinked. "Yes."

John stood. "What?"

"I said, yes. Yes, John, I will marry you. I've missed you so much."

John felt his chest might crack open with joy, considering the happiness that was spilling over inside him. With a cowboy *whoop!* he grabbed Abby around the waist and swept her up in his arms, swinging her around. Suddenly, a cheer and clapping went up around them.

He set her down, looked deep into her eyes, and whispered. "I love you, Abby Cooper. Nothing will change that. Ever. I will take care of you and ours. And there is nothing else in the world I want more."

Abby's tears spilled over. "John. I've loved you right from the beginning."

He didn't waste another minute slipping that big flashy ring on Abby Cooper's finger.

Chapter Twelve

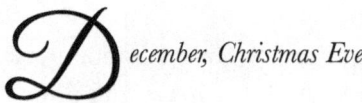ecember, *Christmas Eve*

SNOW FLURRIES FURLED AROUND HIM AS JOHN STOOD LOOKING down at his wife's grave. The kids must have been up here recently and decorated Annie's headstone for Christmas. Their first Christmas without their mother. He sure hoped they would get through the upcoming days unscathed, with so much going on.

The wedding was later tonight.

They'd have Christmas with the children in the morning.

Then tomorrow afternoon, he and Abby would head off for some alone time—a honeymoon, of sorts. Parker and Callie were staying the week with Tom and Sally. Luke would spend Christmas week with his dad.

Some garland and tinsel fluttered in the breeze, catching his attention, and he wondered how long it all would stay put with the winds that kicking up on top of the hill. Looked like they had anchored the wreath and a plastic poinsettia into the ground with wire, so hopefully they would stay put for a while.

He shook his head. His kids never ceased to amaze him.

Glancing up into the gray, overcast sky, he watched a front of darker clouds tumble in from the northwest. There would be more snow by tomorrow. He hoped it held off until he and Abby got to their destination—a cabin he'd rented on the other side of Yellowstone. According to the weather forecasters, there shouldn't be an issue, but you never knew for certain about winter in Montana.

Crouching, he touched Annie's name on the cold marble and traced each letter of her full name. Anne Katherine Parker Rankin. A tear slid down his cheek and he brushed it away before it could freeze there.

"I love you, Annie," he whispered. "I hope I'm doing the right thing. You know I love you with all my heart and always will. I loved you from the first day I saw you after I came back home. That never changed for all the years we were together."

He paused, clearing his throat a little and swiped at his eyes. Taking a deep breath and exhaling, he tried again. "I know you said for me to find someone to be with. Someone to keep me from being lonely. To help me get through life. I know you wanted me to have a partner, like you were to me. But I worry it's too soon. Is it too soon for you, Annie? Do you understand why I need Abby so much?"

He sniffled again, and then stood, hands shoved into his pockets, staring at the ground.

"It's because of you, Annie-girl. I was happy being married, having you as my partner, the mother of my children. I'm happier when I'm part of a couple and you made me see that years ago. All the years I spent alone before you—I don't want that anymore. I need the companionship and the love. I love her, sweetheart. Not like I love you, but just as good. I sure hope you meant what you said because right now, things are in motion, and I wish I just knew for sure that...."

Suddenly, the dark gray clouds above parted and a bright beam of sunshine shot out of a wide patch of blue sky. John looked up and in that sunny patch of bright blue, for just a flash—even if only in his mind's eye—he saw his sweet Annie's angelic face smiling down.

Then he knew. *Thank you, Annie-girl.*

That sunbeam followed him all the way back to the ranch.

~

SIX HOURS LATER....

TO SAY HE WAS AS NERVOUS AS A WHORE IN CHURCH WAS AN understatement.

John Rankin stood outside the side door of the small country church. The chapel was tucked so far back in a valley in the Gallatin Mountain range it took them over an hour to get to it from Rock Creek Ranch. But that small church was where Abby wanted to get married, and so, that is where they would indeed get married.

Snow crystals filtered down around him, blown on a soft breeze from a low-hanging pine bough. He brushed the flakes off his shoulder, then took off his hat and ran a hand over his feverish forehead.

Good Lord. He was sweating like a pig.

Inside, he could hear music and thought that was his cue to step inside the church, but he waited for a minute because that's what he was told to do.

He sure hoped everything went as planned.

The wedding was small by design. Neither he nor Abby saw any reason for a big, fancy affair. Her family drove in from south of Billings the day before—he'd met her parents and sister at the pre-wedding dinner. Tom and Sally came yesterday too. They'd met Abby several weeks earlier, and Tom had given his blessing.

"We just want you to be happy," he'd said, choking a little on his words. John knew he missed his sister.

Of course, his kids and Abby's Luke were there. Buck and Kris, too. He didn't know who else was inside.

The side door creaked open. Parker stuck his head out. "Dad? It's time." But instead of opening the door more fully, he stepped out on the stoop.

John swallowed hard, wondering what his son was up to.

Parker met his gaze and shoved a hand into his jacket pocket. He pulled out an envelope and handed it to John. "It's from me and Callie."

He studied his boy for a moment, then sniffed and opened the flap, pulling out the card.

He stood there, reading it, and damned near fell to pieces right in front of his son.

"You okay, Dad?"

John lifted his gaze and wiped his eyes with the back of his hand. Reaching for Parker, he clutched him to his chest. "I'm fine, son. Just fine."

His children had just given him their blessing—sort of. The card bore personalized messages, one from Callie and one from Parker, telling him how happy they were that he'd found someone to love again, and that they would love Abby too. Of course, Callie's was cryptic and non-committal, but the sentiment was there.

Still, it warmed his heart and meant everything.

"I love you, son. Where is that sister of yours?"

"She's waiting to come down the aisle. We better get inside."

"All right. Lead the way, best man."

Parker grinned and opened the door. John stepped inside and took his place in the front of the vestibule, as instructed the night before at the rehearsal. Parker stepped up to his side.

It was then he spanned the church pews. There were more people than he expected. His gaze drifting, he spied Buck and Kris, and Annie's younger brother, Noah. He wondered where he'd traveled in from. Of course, Tom and Sally were there, too, along with their children, Gage and Olivia.

Luke stood on the other side of Parker. He tossed the boy a glance and winked. His heart warmed when Luke grinned and winked back.

And then the music changed.

Callie stepped into the sanctuary and ambled down the aisle. She smiled big at her father as she took her place in front across from him. She looked so darn pretty in her dress. Grown up. She'd turned twelve this fall. Goodness. He was certain she was wearing makeup that Abby had helped her apply.

God love Abby.

The music changed again. His gaze returned to the back of the church.

Abby stepped into view, her arm linked with her father's, and paused. She wore a knee-length, cream-colored dress, her auburn hair pulled up with tendrils dripping down the sides of her face. She wore pearls on her ears and around her neck. And the sultry smile she had on her face, her gaze pinned on him, made his heart pound.

His bride was stunning. *His bride.* His Abby.

So beautiful. So happy. Mine.

At that moment, the emotion that chased over him nearly dropped John Rankin to his knees. His eyes never left her face as she moved toward him. His heart hammered with each step she took. He'd truly been given a second chance at love, and he was not about to squander it. How he had gotten so lucky, he would never know.

He should let go of the breath he was holding before he passed out.

As Abby handed her bouquet off to Callie, leaning in to give the girl a quick kiss on her cheek, everything in the room went silent—at least to his ears.

He heard nothing. No music. No whispering. No wind outside.

Only his racing heartbeat.

"I am the luckiest man in the world." He took her hands into his and held them tight. "You've never looked more lovely," he whispered.

"And you've never looked so handsome." She tipped her head up and smiled.

John had to steady himself. His knees may buckle yet.

"You're not going to pass out on me, are you?" she murmured.

He tugged her closer. "Not a chance." Then he turned to the minister. "How fast can you do this?"

The reverend smiled. "We gather together this day to unite John Rankin and Abby Cooper in Holy Matrimony…."

Abby's gaze never left his. John didn't let go of her hands the entire ceremony—except to place a gold band on her left finger, right next to that flashy ring.

Epilogue

M *ay 1999*

"OH, ISN'T THAT SIMPLY ADORABLE?"

Abby lifted a pale yellow, hand-crocheted baby blanket out of the perfectly wrapped box. The colors of the wrappings, ribbons, and decorations were yellow, mint green, and white— no blue or pink to be found, because Abby and John didn't want to know the gender of their baby until birth.

"It is adorable. Thank you, Grace!" Glancing at her friend, Abby spread the small blanket out over her lap and fingered the delicate flowers stitched there.

"My mother made it," Grace told her. "She's a whiz with a crochet needle. Sadly, I didn't develop that genetic talent."

"You have other talents." Abby smiled at her.

"That's the last gift!" Callie announced. "Are we ready for cake now?"

Smiling, Abby reached for her stepdaughter's hand. "I think so. Help me up, sweetheart. Please?"

Callie lifted the box off Abby's lap, set it aside, and then reached for Abby. Abby grasped her smaller hands and slowly stood up.

"Oh." Something didn't feel right in her tummy.

Callie leaned in. "Oh goodness. Did I hurt you?"

Abby shook her head. "Oh no. Just getting so big. Let's try again." She laughed the twinge away.

Callie tugged once more.

Abby struggled to her feet and stood there. "Oh. No."

"What?" Callie searched her face.

"Oh dear, Abby." Grace rushed to her side. "Are you okay?"

Looking down, Abby saw the small puddle of water at her feet. She'd already felt the wetness between her legs. "My water broke."

"But you're two weeks early."

Abby nodded. "I know, but the doctor said during my last visit that it could be sooner. Well, here we go."

"Ugh!" Callie jumped back. "Call 9-1-1 someone!"

Abby laughed again and reached for Callie's arm. "No, sweetheart. We don't need to call 9-1-1. Just get your daddy back to the house." Abby knew John was out on the ranch somewhere. She couldn't remember exactly what he said when he left a few hours ago.

"I'm going!" Callie rushed off.

"Try the two-way radio."

"Okay!"

Grace cradled Abby in her arms. "Why don't you sit back down."

"Here's a towel for the chair," someone said. Right now, her brain was spinning, and Abby wasn't sure who. It didn't matter. They were all friends and family here. Maybe it was Sally.

"I'll go get your bag and put it by the door," Grace told her.

"Is it in your room?"

"Yes. By the dresser."

"Got it."

Callie rushed back into the room. "Dad was in the barn. He's coming."

A split-second later, John burst into the great room. "Abby!" He headed for her.

"I'm fine, John."

"I'll carry you to the truck."

"I can walk just fine." She patted his face and smiled.

"Let me help you up."

"That would be lovely, John. Take my hand." His hands were cold and sweaty. She looked him square in the eyes. "John, it's okay. I'm going to be fine."

He held her gaze. "Not sure I am."

"Here's your bag," Grace called out. "I'll follow you out."

They got Abby in the truck, and John behind the wheel, without incident. Abby rolled down her window and looked at Grace. "Call Dr. Simon, please. Tell him I'm coming. And maybe call the hospital too and give them a heads-up. Goodness, I wasn't ready to have a baby today but…."

She didn't finish her sentence because John took off and sped down the dirt road. She rolled up the electric window on her side of the truck to keep out the dust.

"It's okay, John. Slow down. I've got hours to go before —Oh…."

A searing pain encircled her lower back.

"Abby?"

She huffed out a couple of breaths and eased out the word, "Contraction."

"You okay?"

"Just drive. Fast. Oh…." *Another contraction? Too close. Not good. Way too fast.* "The baby. Is. Coming."

"Shit! Don't worry, Abby. I've got this."

She sneered at him. "Just get me to Livingston."

"I've assisted with many births."

"What?" She tried not to panic.

"I mean, I've pulled a lot of calves."

"Good Lord." Abby glared. "John Rankin, I am not a cow!"

"How different could it be?"

"Are you serious?"

He stared back. "Right. I'm driving." The truck tires hit pavement. He turned onto the county road and floored the accelerator.

THE NEXT MORNING, JOHN WALKED THROUGH THE HOSPITAL doors with three children in tow. He held Callie's hand while Parker and Luke followed.

"I still can't believe you delivered the baby on the side of the road, Daddy. That must have been scary. Were cars going by fast?"

"Well, Abby was in the truck, sweetheart. And I'd pulled way over. Plus, the ambulance got there really quick, right after the baby came."

They moved through the lobby and toward the elevator bank.

"Did Abby hurt?"

John glanced down at his daughter. Lately, she'd been obsessed with the pain part of childbirth. He supposed she was thinking of her own future, should she decide to be a mother. She'd been asking Abby a lot of questions about human births, comparing what she knew about cows and horses giving birth.

"I mean," Callie went on, "I know animals don't get medicine and stuff when they are birthing, but people usually do. But Abby didn't because she was on the road. So, did it hurt?"

The elevator doors flew open and all four of them stepped inside. John glanced at Parker, then back to Callie. "She hurt a little, honey. But she's fine. You'll see."

"Okay."

The doors whooshed open again on the second floor, the maternity ward. "This way." He motioned to the right. They walked a few feet down the hall and stopped at Abby's room. Taking a deep breath, he ushered his kids inside.

Abby's face lit up when she saw them.

"Hi kids!"

"You're okay." Callie rushed forward. "Oh. The baby!"

Abby beamed. "Yes, here she is."

John thought he'd never seen Abby look more beautiful, or happy, with their newborn baby cradled into her arms.

"Hi, Mom." Smiling, Luke stepped forward and touched the baby's hand. "She's so little."

"Yes, she is. It's a good thing she has two big brothers to help take care of her."

John watched both boys straighten up and stand a little taller.

Abby looked at Callie. "And a big sister to teach her things."

Callie beamed. "What's her name?"

John sat on the side of the bed and looked at the kids. "We decided early this morning. Kids, meet your baby sister, Finn."

"Finn?" All three chimed at once.

"Like on a fish?" Callie puckered her lips.

"For Finnegan." John chuckled. "Not fish."

Abby continued John's explanation. "My family is Irish," she said. "And I always wanted to keep some of that Irish heritage. Finnegan is a family name, an Irish name. We talked about using it if the baby would be a boy, but then decided since she's a girl, we still like the name."

"She have a middle name?" Callie asked.

"Yes, she does. Finnegan Flora Rankin. Flora was my grandmother's name."

Callie moved closer to the baby. "Well, hello Finnegan Flora. Welcome to the family but stay out of my things. One day I'll teach you to ride. Maybe. Unless you turn out to be a brat."

John cocked a brow and looked at Abby. She sighed deep and grinned back.

"Never a dull moment," he said.

"I wouldn't have it any other way, John Rankin."

DID YOU LOVE *THE RANCHER'S SECOND CHANCE?* HELP OTHERS find this book by leaving a review at your favorite bookstore.

****

Fifteen years later… Want to know how Callie's relationship with her new stepmother develops over the years? What makes Callie leave the ranch after high school, and what brings her back home again a decade later?

And, who is waiting for her when she returns?

Scroll on to read a sneak peek of *CALLIE: Rock Creek Ranch,* Book 2.

CALLIE—Sneak Peek

Manhattan, New York City
  March 2016

"You know I'm proud of you, baby girl, don't you?"

Callie Rankin smiled and closed her eyes at the familiarity of her father's words. She looked forward to their weekly calls, the deep draw of his voice pulling her back home again for a little while.

"I know, Daddy. I work hard. You taught me that." She smiled and pushed back a curtain with one finger, staring out the window of her second-story walk-up. The street below was busy this Sunday morning. She itched to take a walk. The winter had been long and brutal, and this burst of springtime was a welcome change. "I love my job. There's talk of a promotion if I play my cards right."

"You got that strong Rankin work ethic in you, that's for sure," he said.

She did. It had served her well in the rodeo days of her youth and continued to be an asset in her career. That work ethic was important to her. "That's very true, Daddy." *And I owe it all to you.*

There was a brief pause, and then her father continued, changing the subject. "Sugar sure could use a good run around those barrels."

"Sugar's getting a little old for that, Daddy. Me, too."

The thought of her quarter horse, though, sent a slight spiral of homesickness into her belly. "I miss her. I would stable her here, but that's impossible and she wouldn't be happy. Besides, I work a lot of late nights and I don't know when I could ride her."

"Your life sure has changed."

He always said that, as if it was a surprise—like her leaving was just yesterday. Fact was, it was coming up on ten years since she'd left Rock Creek Ranch for college. It was his way of saying *she* had changed. "I'm still the same Callie, though," she teased. "I can give you a run for your money any day of the week."

He laughed, and she savored his bellow. It was good to hear him laugh.

"Montana misses you something awful, baby girl."

Translation: *He* missed her something awful. She knew he did. It wasn't Sugar, or Montana, it was him. "I'll be home soon, Daddy."

"When?"

Reaching into her bag, she pulled out her planner. She was the only one of her friends who still carried a paper planner and didn't record everything on her cell. Phone tucked between her chin and shoulder, she sifted through the pages. "Let me see when I can get away. Maybe July or August."

"It's been two years, girl. You realize that?"

"What?" Certainly not. "I'm sure it's been—"

"Nope. Two years since last Christmas. So, it's been almost two and a half."

Oh, dear. She flipped a few more pages. "August. I'll come in August, Daddy. Promise." She could almost see his nod.

"August is good," he said. "Your mama's birthday and all. Maybe we'll ride up to the family plot."

Callie's eyes immediately stung. She reached for the locket around her neck and fiddled with it—a simple gold locket her father had one time given to her mother. Now it was hers. "I'd like that a lot," she told him, trying not to sniffle.

"Me, too. So, I'm expecting you now, girl. Got that? A Rankin doesn't back down on her word. I can't wait to see you in August." He paused and then added. "But if you can come before then, it sure would be good. Got some things to talk about."

Something prickled in her chest. *Oh?* "Daddy, is everything okay?" Immediately, her thoughts turned to family. Something was going on, she could tell by the tone of his voice. Was it Abby, her stepmother? Or was something going on with one of her siblings—Parker, Finn, or Luke?

"Everything is fine, sweetheart." He snorted. "Just some business about the ranch that I want to go over with you and Parker. You know, one day, the old Parker homestead section of Rock Creek Ranch will belong to the two of you."

She wished he wouldn't talk like that.

Maybe it was his tone, or maybe it was something heavy in her heart, but things were suddenly off. His mood had shifted from *happy to talk to you* to *serious shit* on a dime. That prickle morphed into a trigger of worry and curled up under her breastbone. How could she tell him she never intended to run the ranch with Parker? He knew that, deep down, didn't he?

But her father was a stubborn Alpha rancher used to getting his way.

He continued. "And you need to be prepared, Callie-girl, for me to convince you to stay."

"Daddy, you know—"

"I gotta run now. Time for me to get out of the kitchen and into the saddle."

She glanced at her watch. Seven o'clock in the morning there. Didn't matter that it was a Sunday. *Ranch work never ends.* "Okay, Daddy. Give my love to the others. Abby too. Love you and talk soon."

"Love you more, baby girl. Love you more. And if you find you can come home sooner, I hope you do."

He clicked off the phone before she did. With a sigh, she sat by the window and looked down at her planner, now in her lap. She fished a pen out of her bag and wrote the word "Montana" in big block letters across the month of August.

She stared at the word for a moment.

No more skirting it, no excuses. She was going home. And perhaps he was right—she should find a way to get there before August.

Beneath the word Montana, she made a list:

- Check vacation days at work and schedule.
- Get airfare.
- Book rental vehicle.
- Get head on straight.

Going home to Montana meant a lot of things. It meant facing family she hadn't seen or interacted with much for far too long. It meant being civil to her stepmother, and that was always a challenge. It meant having the hard conversations with her daddy that she didn't want to have about the ranch and her future. His future too.

And it meant she would see Murphy Reynolds.

Yellowstone River Roundup, Montana Fair
  Billings, Montana, August 2006

Not a thought ran through Callie Rankin's head as she leaned up on Sugar's neck to gain speed. Every fiber of her being concentrated on one task—horse and rider moving as one around the cloverleaf. Relieved they'd gotten around the tricky second barrel without error, they sped toward the final one. Callie focused on keeping her hands in position. Pushing back in the saddle and sitting on her pockets, she approached the third turn.

Murphy's voice burst through her concentration, guiding her. She'd heard his words a million times.

Stay two-handed. Look past the barrel. Find your spot.

Don't start the turn too early.

Wait. Wait. Keep low.

There you go. Leg even with the barrel. Drop your hand. Saddle horn.

Squeeze with your inside leg. Let Sugar do the rest.

They burst out of the third turn, barrel upright, and her quarter horse raced toward the line. The crowd exploded. Her heart danced in her chest.

Did she beat the best time?

Callie pulled up to a fast stop between the gates and turned her horse into the pen to her right. She looked up at the timer.

Fourteen-point-one-two seconds. Her best time ever.

I might have done it!

One more rider to go and she could win. Her daddy would be so pleased!

Giddy inside, she searched through the faces at the back of the arena. She urged Sugar forward and finally spotted Murphy Reynolds standing by the rear gate. She cantered toward him.

Tall and slender, he leaned his backside against the fence,

arms loosely crossed over his chest. Tan from the sun and ranch work, his dark forearms showed below the turned-back cuffs of his starched western shirt. His hat sat square on his head and beneath that white brim, his dark gaze fixed on her.

He smiled. Callie pulled Sugar up in front of him and grinned back.

"I think you did it," he drawled.

"This might be my night."

Unable to contain her excitement any longer, Callie slid from the horse. As soon as her boots hit the dirt, she was moving forward. Fast. Murphy pushed off the fence and they drew together, like magnets.

Her arms went around his neck. "Thank you so much, Murphy. I couldn't have done it without you."

He swept her into his arms and swung her around. She giggled like a little girl.

When her feet hit the ground again, everything swirled to a sudden stop. The whirlwind of the past thirty seconds abruptly halted and Murphy's gaze—those dark, soul-filled eyes of his—captured hers and held. For that moment, Callie wasn't the rancher's daughter anymore, and he wasn't the ranch hand. He wasn't the guy who pushed her to run harder, take the barrels tighter. Nor was he the person she often confided in when things got tough with her stepmother or siblings. Or when it felt like her daddy was ignoring her.

And she wasn't just any cowgirl. She was more. Something else was going on. Something awkward and irresistible and unnerving, all at once.

Murphy leaned in and a foreign zing moved up through Callie's chest, almost taking her breath. Her heart thumped madly.

"Murphy," she whispered.

But she didn't have time to finish her thought as his lips descended and brushed hers.

That mere touch lit a spark inside Callie that she didn't know what to do with. She pushed back before the kiss could go any further.

"Murphy, don't."

He shook his head, as if to pull himself out of a trance, and his hands dropped to his sides. "Callie, I'm sorry. I…."

"It's okay." She turned and grasped Sugar's reins. "I need to get back—"

Another cheer went up from the crowd. Callie's gaze shot to the timer. Thirteen-point-nine-six.

Shit.

Tonight was not her night after all.

A couple of hours later, Callie sat in the passenger side of the truck while Murphy drove. They'd left Billings twenty minutes earlier and were on their way back to Rock Creek. Twenty minutes of silence was a long time in the close quarters of the truck cab, but it was time enough for Callie to sit and think about what had almost happened earlier. And they had a lot of empty minutes to fill ahead of them. The tension was thick as butter.

He'd wanted to kiss her.

And she'd nearly let him.

Callie wanted to think it had all come about unexpectedly. That it was an impromptu, impulsive kind of thing on Murphy's behalf. But she knew it wasn't. Things had been changing, building between them for a while.

The lingering touches. The flirts. The over the shoulder grins.

Glancing at him, she studied his profile. His jaw was set. He was thinking, too.

She had to cut this off at the pass. "I'm leaving in two weeks, Murphy."

He stared straight ahead. She watched his lips thin out a little. Then he nodded. "Yep."

"It's college. It's what I need to do."

"Yep."

"Is that all you are going to say?"

In one quick motion, Murphy swerved the truck to a pull-off at the side of the road and parked. He turned and looked at her, his left arm draped over the steering wheel. "What do you want me to say, Callie?"

She was taken aback. His stare was intense, and every inch of it made her heart beat a little faster. If she had half a brain, she would rush into his arms again and let him kiss her silly. And if he did—if she let that happen—she knew everything she'd planned for herself would suddenly change.

Everything.

She would stay. They'd be a couple. And she'd be stuck in Montana, and her miserable insignificant life, for the rest of her days.

"I'm going to college," she told him. "I'm leaving the ranch."

He didn't miss a beat. "Callie, I… Please. Let's talk. I am falling in love—"

He cut off the last words and she was glad.

He was older. Twenty-five years to her eighteen. He was ready to settle down. Get married. Have kids.

She wasn't. Not yet.

Would he wait for her?

No. That was unfair. To them both.

The tension in her jaw was almost painful. The intense look in his eyes was even more so. "No, Murphy," she whispered. "Don't. Don't fall in love with me. You deserve someone who wants what you want—a life here. On the ranch. I'm not that girl. I have plans. There is nothing to talk about."

"There's no one else, Callie. Not for me."

The crack in his voice was almost her undoing.

Callie shook her head. *Please don't make this difficult.* "No, Murphy. I'm leaving. Two weeks. And I don't know when I'll be back." *Or if I'll be back.* "You need to forget about me and live your life."

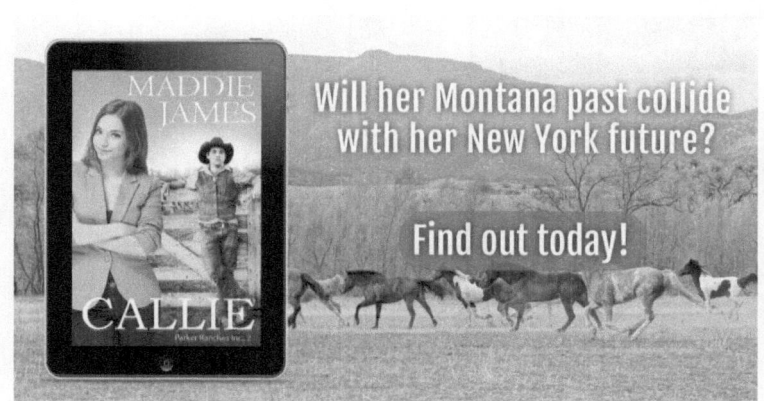

Insider News

Do you get my Insider News?

Be the first to get the latest news about my books—new releases, free ebooks, sales and discounts, sneak peeks, and exclusive content! Just add your email address at this link:

https://maddiejamesbooks.com/pages/newsletter

Bonus! I'll send you a FREE ebook for signing up.
(This deal is ONLY for new newsletter subscribers!)

Maddie James' Rancher Books

Rock Creek Ranch
The Rancher's Second Chance (Book 1)
Callie (Book 2)
Parker (Book 3)
Leaving Noah (Book 4)

Watch for:
Finn's Lawman (Book 5)
Abby's Secret (Book 6)

Branded Filly Ranch
Corporate Cowboy (Book 1)
Protecting Sarah (Book 2)

Watch for:
Saving Amanda (Book 3)

Sweet Grass Ranch
Ethan: Black Sheep Cowboy (Book 1)
Evan: Kiss Me Again, Cowboy (Book 2)

Watch for:

Aiden: The Cowboy's Baby (Book 3)
Aaron: Marry Me, Cowboy (Book 4)

Remington Ranches (Texas & Kentucky)

Jake's Temptation (Book 1)

Suggested Reading Order

Linked by strong family relationships, these rancher stories take place in multiple ranch settings in Montana (Rankin's Rock Creek Ranch; The Branded Filly Ranch), South Dakota (Sweet Grass Ranch), Texas and Kentucky (Remington Ranches).

It's not easy. Relationships get in the way. Egos sometimes, too. But at the very core of their existence, is home, family, and love.

These books are romance stories with happily-ever-after endings. Some are sweet, most are steamy, and a few are romantically erotic. *(Please review product descriptions prior to purchase.)*

Suggested Reading Order Across the Series, Currently Available Books

The Rancher's Second Chance, Rock Creek Ranch 1
Callie, Rock Creek Ranch 2
Callie's Wedding, Rock Creek Ranch 2.5

Parker, Rock Creek Ranch 3
Corporate Cowboy, Branded Filly Ranch 1
Protecting Sarah, Branded Filly Ranch 2
Jake's Temptation, Remington Ranch 1
Ethan: Black Sheep Cowboy, Sweet Grass Ranch 1
Leaving Noah, Rock Creek Ranch 4
Evan: Kiss Me Again, Cowboy, Sweet Grass Ranch 2

Learn more at www.maddiejamesbooks.com

About Maddie James

Whether writing flirty contemporary romance or gritty romantic suspense, Maddie James writes to silence the people in her head.

In 2022, Maddie celebrated her 25th year of publishing romance fiction under multiple pen names. Her collective body of work includes over 70 titles. Maddie loves writing small town contemporary romance and cowboy worlds. As M.L. Jameson, she pens paranormal and romantic suspense. When writing short erotic fiction as M. J. Ames, her writing is basically, well, naughty.

Affair de Coeur says Maddie, "shows a special talent for traditional romance," and RT Book Reviews claimed, "James deftly combines romance and suspense, so hope on for an exhilarating ride."

Read more: https://maddiejamesbooks.com/pages/about